CAUGHT!

That guy was the dogcatcher, see, and when he got out of his pickup and started creeping toward me with a butterfly net, I began to suspect that I was in the wrong place at the wrong time.

"Hold still, doggie," he said. "Just two more steps and I'll take you for a little ride."

Who did he think he was talking to? I mean, how dumb would you have to be to fall for that "hold still doggie" business? I showed him a few fangs and gave him a growl, and fellers, he dropped that butterfly net and flew back into the pickup.

"Mobile three to city hall! Larry, he attacked me, almost got my leg, for gosh sakes send some police and the ambulance, this mutt has hydrophobia, I ain't kidding!"

It's a Dog's Life

HANK THE COWDOG

John R. Erickson

Illustrations by Gerald L. Holmes

Maverick Books, Inc.

MAVERICK BOOKS, INC.
Published by Maverick Books, Inc.
P.O. Box 549, Perryton, TX 79070
Phone: 806.435.7611
www.hankthecowdog.com

First published in the United States of America by Maverick Books, Inc. 1984,
Texas Monthly Press, 1988, and Gulf Publishing Company, 1990.
Subsequently published simultaneously by Viking Children's Books and Puffin
Books, members of Penguin Putnam Books for Young Readers, 1999.
Currently published by Maverick Books, Inc., 2011.

5 7 9 10 8 6 4

LIBRARY OF CONGRESS CATALOGING-IN-PUBLICATION DATA
Erickson, John R.
It's a dog's life / John R. Erickson ; illustrations by Gerald L. Holmes.
p. cm.
Originally published in series: Hank the Cowdog ; 3.
Summary: Duped into thinking the world is coming to an end,
Hank the Cowdog winds up in town for some more adventures including
getting in and out of a case of "soap hydrophobia."
ISBN 978-1-59188-103-2 (pbk. ; alk. paper)
[1. Dogs—Fiction. 2. West (U.S.)—Fiction. 3. Humorous stories.
4. Mystery and detective stories.] I. Holmes, Gerald L., ill. II. Title.
III. Series: Erickson, John R. Hank the Cowdog ; 3.
PZ7.E72556It 1999 [fic]—dc21 98-41811 CIP AC

Printed in the United States of America

*I dedicate this story to the kids of my
tribe: the little Sparkses, Dykemas, Ericksons,
Marmadukes, Pattersons, and Harters.*

CONTENTS

CHAPTER ONE

The End
of the World

It's me again, Hank the Cowdog. One morning
around ten o'clock Drover brought me some
incredible news. He said the world was coming to
an end.

I had gotten in from work around daylight,
washed up in the septic tank, and hit my
gunnysack just as the sun peeked over that big
cottonwood tree down by the creek. It had been a
slow night but still I was bushed. Must have been
the accumulation of long nights. This security
work begins to wear on a guy after a while.

I had given Drover the night off, so by the time
I came dragging in he was all fresh and ready to
go exploring or some such foolishness. He asked
if I wanted to go with him.

1

"No sir, I certainly don't, and here's the rest of it. I plan to be sound asleep when the mailman comes by. You get your little self up there by the mailbox and give him a good barking. You got that?"

The smile left his face. "Okay Hank, but I sure did want to go exploring."

"That exploring can keep for another day, son." I scratched my gunnysack until it was fluffed up just the way I like it, then I flopped down. What a beautiful feeling! "We tend to business first, Drover, and then if there's any time left, we tend to pleasure. Why do I have to keep telling you that?"

"I don't know, Hank. I forget things."

I looked at the runt and shook my head. "You forget things. How can you forget that the mailman comes by here every day at the same time? How can you forget that one of our most important jobs is to bark at him? How can you forget that you're wasting my time and I'm ready to go to sleep?" I noticed that he was staring at my ear. "What are you staring at?"

"You got three fleas crawling on your ear."

They were coming out of my bed. Derned gunnysack was getting a little ripe and needed changing. You'd think the cowboys would notice something like that and give me a fresh cake sack

every six months or so, but they can sell 'em back to the Co-op for a nickel apiece, see, and that sort of puts a price on my services.

You never really know these ranch folks until there's a nickel involved. Give the Head of Ranch Security a five-cent bed every six months? No siree, not with cattle prices the way they are. That new gunnysack just might take the ranch down into bankruptcy.

So if you want to know why my bed was full of fleas, there's your answer. It had nothing to do with my personal hygiene. I bathe in the sewer every single day, I make a sincere effort to keep the sandburs out of my tail, I scratch every flea that shows himself.

In other words, I'm one of the cleanest dogs I ever met except Beulah the collie, and oh, just the mention of her name makes my heart start whammming around in my chest!

How could she love a bird dog when she could have me? What did Plato have that I didn't have? I'll answer that question. Plato was so homely, so pitiful, so incompetent that Beulah felt sorry for him. That's all I could figger. I mean, in a contest of looks, brains, courage, brute strength, or anything else you'd want to mention, Plato came in dead last.

How did I get started on Beulah? I can't let myself do that and what the heck was I talking about?

I can't remember.

Okay, I've got it now. Fleas. I was discussing fleas. It doesn't matter how careful you are with your personal hygiene, if the ranch executives are too tight to give you a clean gunnysack every six months or so, you're going to by George come up with fleas, and Drover was correct in saying that I had three of the little devils crawling on my left ear.

Know what I did? I got my hind leg up and went to kicking them fleas, and fellers, I wouldn't want to be a flea in that situation because my hind legs are very powerful and my claws are just death on fleas.

"I think you got 'em," said Drover. "I hope they don't get into my bed."

"Son, when this dog takes after a flea, it needs more than a bed. It needs a cemetery, and that goes for larger animals too. Now I'm going to sleep. Tell me what your assignment is."

He twisted his mouth around and squinted one eye. "Uh . . . let's see . . ."

"Mailman."

"Mailman. Mail-MAN. MAIL-man."

"Bark."

"Bark." He shook his head.

"Bark at."

"Bark at . . . bark at . . . mailman bark at . . . bark at the mailman!"

"Very good, Drover. Now, keep saying that to yourself and run up to the road before you forget again."

"Okay, Hank, bark at the mailman." He started

off but stopped. "Hank, how come we bark at the mailman?"

I stared at him. "Are you asking why we bark at the mailman?"

"Yeah. If he brings the mail, how come we bark at him?"

"Holy cats, Drover, at your age you're still asking a question like that? Son, if you don't know the answer by this time, it wouldn't do any good for me to tell you. Now go on before I lose my temper."

"Okay, Hank. Bark at the mailman, bark at the mailman." And off he went to the mailbox.

I settled into my gunnysack and released my grip on the world. But you know what? I couldn't fall asleep for a long time. I kept asking myself, "Why DO we bark at the mailman?"

If you look at it in a certain light, it really doesn't make much sense. As far back as I can remember, no mailman has ever killed a chicken, robbed a nest, broke into a sack of feed, or done anything worse than deliver the mail.

But that right there is one of the primary dangers of having an active, superior type of intelligence. On the one hand, it's necessary for security work. On the other hand, it can come up with foolish questions. Ma used to say that back at the beginning of time, God built a thousand questions but only two hundred and fifty answers, so there you are.

Why do we bark at the mailman? Because, by George, cowdogs have always barked at the mailman and they always will.

And with that out of the way, I went to sleep.

It was wonderful, delicious. Geeze, I love sleep. Nothing gives me more pleasure than to lie there with my paws in the air and have dreams that make me twitch. I don't know what it is that makes twitching dreams special, but they're the very best kind.

So there I was, twitching and rolling my eyes and at peace with the world, dreaming of fresh bloody bones and . . . well, Beulah, when all at once I heard a high-pitched squeal.

"Hank, oh Hank, it's awful, wake up, I'm so scared I can't stand it, wake up!"

One eye popped open. It was a short-haired, stub-tailed white dog, and he was jumping up and down. "Bzelwykqe dkeithsle pclkenck qghbnesl," I said.

"What?"

My other eye slid open. "These are my fresh bloody bones and next week's an entirely different matter."

He twisted his head and looked at me. "What are you talking about, Hank?"

I pushed myself up and staggered over against the gas tank. My head began to clear. "What's the meaning of this?"

"The meaning of what, Hank?"

"The meaning of . . . I don't know. Whatever it is we're talking about."

"You mean . . . bloody bones?"

"Okay, stop right there. Whose bones and why are they bloody? Try to remember every detail. Reconstruct the scene of the crime just as you saw it. So far, we've only got one clue: the bones are bloody. What kind of bones were they?"

"Uh . . . fresh bloody bones."

"Very good. That's two clues: fresh and bloody. Now you've got to concentrate. *Whose bones were they?*"

Drover rolled his eyes. I could tell he was trying to concentrate. "I guess they're yours, Hank. I haven't seen 'em yet."

"What are you talking about?"

"Well . . . I'm not sure."

"Then *what is the meaning of this conversation*? Why am I standing here?"

"I don't know, Hank. Maybe you better sit down."

I sat down and took a deep breath. "Drover, I was asleep and you woke me up. Why did you wake me up?"

"Oh. Oh-h-h-h-h Hank, I just heard the awful news and I thought you ought to know!"

"What awful news?"

The little mutt was shivering all over by this time. "Oh Hank, the world's going to come to an end tomorrow at three o'clock!"

"HUH? The world . . . three o'clock . . . that's impossible!"

"No, it's true, I know it's true! Oh, I'm scared, Hank. This has never happened to me before!"

Just then, Sally May came out of the house, jumped into her car, and went roaring out of the driveway, throwing up gravel and dust. She turned left at the country road and headed west toward town.

Drover's eyes got as big as plates. "There, you see that? She must have heard the news."

Well, this was, shall we say, shocking. We didn't have much time to prepare. Furthermore, how do you prepare for the end of the world? As I was sifting through the various options, I heard a commotion up around the house.

It was Pete the Barncat. He was jumping up in the air and rolling around on the ground and yowling. It appeared that he'd taken the fits.

"Come on, Drover, we'd better check this out."

We ran up the hill. Something terrible was happening on the ranch and I had to find out what it was.

The Thick
Plottens

When we got to the top of the hill we found
Pete rolling around in the dirt in front of
the yard gate. I studied the scene and came up
with an explanation for his odd behavior: he had
choked on a chicken bone.

I couldn't think of anyone who deserved it
more than Pete, and yet there's a heart beating
inside this massive body of mine and every now
and then it can be touched by tragedy. I kind of
hated to be there, watching Pete in his last
moments of life.

Drover went up to him. Pete was on his back,
kicking all four paws in the air and rolling his
eyes. "What's wrong, Pete?"

He quit twitching and looked up at Drover.

"The end of the world is coming! I can feel it."

Drover glanced at me. "Did you hear that?"

"I heard it but I don't believe it. Step aside and let me check this thing out." I pushed Drover out of the way and stood over the cat. "I'm going to order this cat to open his mouth. When he does, we'll find a chicken bone caught in his throat.

"This is a classic case of greed, Drover, which is very common in cats. I recognized the signs the minute I got here. They get to thinking they can eat anything and the first thing you know

12

they get choked on a bone. Now watch. Open your mouth, cat."

He opened his mouth. Drover and I looked inside. I spotted two tonsils and the little punching bag that hangs in front of the throat. No bone.

I stepped back. "I was afraid of that. Sometimes the bone . . ."

"It's not a bone, Hank," said Pete in an eerie voice. "I can feel the end of the world coming."

Drover gasped. "Hank, he said it again! Oh my gosh! What are we going to do?"

"First, we don't panic. Second, we interrogate this cat. And third . . . we look for the third point in our plan of action." I went back to Pete. "Exactly what makes you think the world's coming to an end?"

"Cat's intuition."

"I don't believe in cat's intuition. There's no way to test it."

"Yes there is. Just ask me any question about the end of the world."

"All right." I paced back and forth. "What day is it due?"

"Tomorrow."

"What time of day?"

"Three o'clock."

"Hmmm." His answers matched Drover's

report. When you get the same answers from two different sources, you have to take it seriously. And then there was Sally May rushing away from the house. That had been pretty suspicious too.

Pete lay there with his eyes closed. "I know how you can check it for sure."

"Well, by George let's hear it, and be quick about it."

"You have to say please."

I chuckled at that. "Me, say please to a cat? Do you realize you are speaking to the Head of Ranch Security? I will not say please to a cat—ever."

I bent my head down and showed him some fangs—growled, narrowed my eyes, raised the hair on the back of my neck as well as all the way down my spine, gave him the whole nine yards of threatening gestures. And as you might expect, he changed his mind.

"Well, maybe I will tell you."

"You bet you will, and you'll tell the truth and nothing but the truth. So start talking while I still have myself under control."

When a cat has some running room or a tree to climb, he'll talk trash and very seldom will you hear him tell the truth. But put one flat on his back on the ground, stand over him with some deadly fangs, and fellers, you can make a Christian out of any cat. I guarantee it.

Well, we finally got the truth out of him. I don't know why he didn't tell the truth in the first place. It would have been so much simpler and easier for all of us, but cats are just that way. They seem to get a kick out of being deceitful. It's just part of their nature.

Under severe questioning Pete finally confessed about where he'd learned that the world was coming to an end. Just as I had suspected, it had nothing to do with so-called "cat's intuition." He'd been sitting on the window sill when Sally May got a phone call. He'd listened to the conversation (it's called eavesdropping and cats are very good at it) and he'd seen her write this message down on her calendar: "End of the world, 3:00 p.m."

I glanced at Drover. "Well, there's the scoop on this end-of-the-world business. Now all we have to do is check the calendar. Of course there's one small problem."

"Sure is."

"And what is that small problem, Drover?"

He gave me a blank stare. "I was just asking myself that same question."

"The small problem is that we have to get into the house because that's where the calendar is.

Come on, son, we've got work to do." I turned to Pete. "You can leave, cat, but don't go far. We may have some more questions for you later on."

Pete gave me a very strange smile and went up toward the machine shed, twitching the end of his tail. I watched him for a long time. I didn't like that smile. There was just something about it that made me suspicious.

But we had work to do. Drover and I jumped the fence and began circling the house, looking for a way to get inside. All at once I heard an odd noise. I stopped.

"Hold it! What's that?" We listened. There it was again, a clicking sound. "It's a time bomb, Drover! Red Alert! Run for your life!"

We dashed around to the front yard and hid behind that big hackberry tree there by the porch. I waited for the blast, and in the silence I heard that same clicking sound—right beside me.

My ears, which are very sensitive scientific instruments, followed the sound and traced it to Drover. "Why are your teeth chattering?"

"What?"

"I said, why are your teeth chattering? And how can I conduct an investigation with you making noise?"

"Oh. I'm sorry, Hank. I guess I'm scared about

the end of the world."

I shook my head and walked a few steps away. "I don't know, Drover, sometimes I just think you're not worth the dadgum effort. How many times have I told you that a cowdog has to be fearless?"

He hung his head. "I know, you've told me but . . . it's the end of the world, Hank."

"Maybe it is and maybe it ain't. At this point it's merely a suppository proposition and all we've got to go on is circumscribal evidence. We won't know for sure until we get into the house and check Sally May's calendar. Now, are you going to help with this investigation or do I have to send you down to the gas tanks for the rest of the day?"

He thought it over. "I guess I'll go down to the gas tanks."

"Oh no you won't."

"I guess I'll stay here."

"That's more like it. Drover, always remember this: it ain't the size of the dog in the fight that matters; it's the size of the fog in the dog. That's what life is all about."

He stared at me and then nodded his head. "I'd wondered . . . what was it all about."

"Now listen very carefully." I looked all around to be sure we were alone. "We've got no choice but

17

to make a penetration into the house."

"A what?"

"A penetration. We'll make a small slit in that window screen and one of us will go inside."

"Which one?"

"We'll decide that when the time comes. You ready to move out?" He gulped and nodded. "All right, let's go."

We slipped away from the tree and sneaked up to one of the south windows. The window was open. All we had to do was get past the screen.

A lot of people think that you can keep a dog out by locking the doors. That's not true. A cowdog who is highly skilled in penetration techniques can approach your ordinary window screen, make a small hole with one of his teeth, and then slit the screen.

I began the procedure—went up on my hind legs, poked one of my large front teeth through the screen, and made a slashing upward motion with my head.

The screen fell off and one corner of it hit Drover between the eyes. He yelped. "Sorry, Drover, but as you can see the screen was improperly installed. Typical cowboy job. But never mind. There's our open window. We're ready to make the penetration. I'll go inside and you stand guard. If you see anything suspicious, give me the code word: Mayday. You got that?"

He nodded.

"Now remember: pay attention, don't go to sleep, and keep your eyes open. The future of the entire world depends on us, Drover."

"What if we mess up?"

"That gets into the realm of the unthinkable. There's no margin for error. We've never played for bigger stakes. So, until we meet again . . ."

I patted him on the shoulder, coiled my legs, and leaped through the window.

CHAPTER THREE

Playing for Big Steaks

Why would anyone put a cactus plant right under a window? In fact, why would anyone want a dadgum cactus plant in the house?

Cactus is a scourge. Out in the pasture you have to put up with it because it's there. But why would anyone dig one up and bring it into the house? I can guarantee that no dog would do such a silly thing.

As you might have guessed by now, Sally May had parked a cactus plant right under the window. I saw it as I cleared the window sill, tried to alter course in mid-air, but by then it was too late. Hit right in the middle of the sucker and fellers, it hurt. And I squalled.

Drover must have heard me. "Oh my gosh,

what is it, Hank, mayday, mayday, help, run, they're after us Hank. I'll meet you at the machine shed!"

He was halfway across the yard and taking aim for the machine shed when I called him back. "Get yourself back here and stand your ground!"

He came back. "Okay, Hank, but I thought . . ."

"You thought you'd save your own skin and leave me in here without a guard, is what you thought. That's very close to treason, Drover. Don't let it happen again."

He took up his position under the window and I went on with my investigation, which was none too easy since I had cactus spines in my brisket and front paws. It's not easy to limp on both feet at once.

The house was quiet except for the ticking of a clock. I crept through the living room, past a pair of High Loper's dirty socks and a recent issue of the *West Texas Livestock Weekly*.

Near the center of the room I paused to study some photographs on the wall. There was one of Loper, another of Sally May, and another of the two of them together. Why do humans always grin in their photographs?

I moved on, stuck my head into the bedroom, checked it out. Sally May had made the bed before she left in such a rush. That's the kind of important clue you look for.

The trouble with clues is that you have to figure out what they mean. For instance:

1) Sally May had made her bed because she knew the end of the world was coming and she didn't want the world to end with her bed unmade.

2) She had made her bed because she thought the world *wasn't* coming to an end. If she'd thought the end of the world was coming, she wouldn't have cared what her bed looked like.

3) She made her bed every day regardless of what the rest of the world was doing.

So there you are, a little insight into the kind of heavy analysis that goes into an investigation.

I tiptoed into the kitchen and started looking around for the telephone. According to Pete's testimony, Sally May had written on her calendar while she was talking on the phone. Hence, the calendar had to be close to the phone.

I was studying the layout of the room, when, all at once, I caught an unusual scent. I had a hunch that it needed checking out. It just might prove to be the missing piece of the puzzle.

I sniffed the air until I got my parameters and followed the scent through a door and out to the utility room. The scent grew stronger. I knew I was getting close. This was no ordinary scent. In my many years of security work, I had never encountered a smell quite like this one.

I went to the center of the room and took another reading. With no conscious effort on my part, my nose turned fifteen degrees to the left and stopped, then lowered seven degrees and stopped. You might say that my nose had traced out invisible crosshairs and had found the target.

I felt myself moving, propelled by an unknown and mysterious force. At times like this I become a weapon, an instrument guided by secret powers that are known only to the top echelon of cowdogs.

Experts have estimated that there are only three cowdogs in the entire world who have this kind of ability, and I guess I don't need to point out that I'm one of them. It's a real honor to be listed in the Top Three, but as I've said many times before, greatness without grace is mere vanity, so a guy needs to work on his humility even though he's been listed in the Top Three.

I crept forward. The scent grew stronger. It was indeed a remarkable smell. It wasn't a skunk, it wasn't a badger, it wasn't a coyote, it wasn't a coon. But I had a suspicion that it belonged to an animal of some kind, perhaps a species I had never encountered before. And whatever it was, it had powerful musk glands.

Up ahead, I saw two objects in a corner behind the back door. The room was dark and I was relying pretty much on instruments, you might say, which means that I couldn't see very well.

But as I drew closer I began to get visual readings. These creatures were built in the shape of an L, a strange configuration to say the least. They had leathery skin and no hair. And unless my eyes deceived me, they had no legs. How they managed to walk with no legs I didn't know, but then it wasn't my job at that point to explain such things.

But here's the real shocker, and you might want to get a good grip on your chair. *They were headless.* Yes sir, no heads, just long necks.

I had no way of knowing whether they were hostile or friendly, and in my business a guy learns not to take chances. We usually attack and ask questions later. I mean, you can always apologize if you've erred on the side of toughness, whereas a mistake in the other direction can lead to grave consequences—and I mean *grave* as in shallow grave or unmarked grave.

Three feet away from the enemy I stopped and took a final reading. The scent was very strong. It

smelled bad. You might even say it w

The creatures hadn't moved. They
huddled there in the shadows, staring
stared back. Never let an enemy stare y
Show the slightest bit of weakness or in
in your eyes and they'll get you.

It was time to attack. I coiled my legs
me and flew through the air, buried both
under my weight, knocked 'em to the floor.
must have released their musk because I c
hardly stand the smell.

I fought and slashed until I felt their bodies
limp. Then I stepped back and was a litt
surprised that there wasn't any blood on the floo
But what surprised me even more . . .

I don't know how to say this. It was a simple
case of mistaken identity. It could have happened
to any dog, and remember that it was very dark
on the back porch.

What I'm driving at is that the creatures
turned out to be an old smelly pair of High
Loper's cowboy boots. Why Sally May allowed
them in her house I don't know, but I can't take
the blame for that. I mean, I was doing my job
and . . . never mind.

You'd think that when a pair of boots got that
old and rank, somebody would throw them away.

Well, I'd wasted some valuable time. I had to get back to my investigation. I went into the kitchen. I was in the process of checking out the walls and conducting a search for the phone and calendar when I caught another scent—the kind that makes your mouth water.

My ears shot up and my eyes got big and I went to sniffing the floor, the cabinets, under the dinner table, and the more I smelled the better I liked it. It was driving me nuts, it smelled good.

At last I went up on my hind legs and looked on top of the table. And there they were: three of the biggest, thickest, juiciest, most bodacious delicious looking T-bone steaks I'd ever seen.

Sally May had put 'em out on the table to thaw.

Just then I heard Drover. "Hank, is anything wrong? Hurry up, I'm getting scared!"

I went through the house and stuck my head out the window. "Relax, son, everything's going according to plan. I'm still conducting my investigation, but it turns out that we're playing for bigger steaks than I thought. It'll take me another ten minutes to get all the data, uh, digested."

"Is the world going to end tomorrow?"

"I'm still working on that, Drover. Just be patient. Stay at your post and keep a sharp lookout."

I left him and returned to the kitchen. I wasn't sure I could eat three whole steaks at one sitting. I mean, when a guy eats nothing but Co-op dog food for years and years, his stomach shrinks. But I'm no quitter.

I went up on my hind legs and started chewing on the first steak. It was half-frozen and not the easiest thing to chew, but I seem to thrive on adversity. While I was chewing on it, the plate fell off the table. It hit the floor and busted into a dozen pieces, and blood splattered all over the place.

That was okay. Before Sally May came back, I'd have the floor shined up and she'd never be any the wiser.

You know, when a guy's been on Co-op dog food most of his life, he can sort of lose his head over a T-bone steak. That first steak was outstanding. I was chewing up the last bite, had my mouth plumb full of beef, when Drover sounded the alarm.

"Hank! Mayday! Mayday! Sally May turned at the mailbox and she's heading this way! Oh my gosh, do something, Hank!"

Had to swaller that bite before I could answer, danged near strangled myself as it was so big. "I'll be right with you, Drover. Let me get a few more details under my belt and I'll be done."

I tore into the next steak. I had the time element figgered down to the last second. Sally May would pull up to the back door. When I heard the car door slam, I'd run to the front of the house, dive through the window, and disappear into the sunset, so to speak.

I wasn't about to leave those steaks unattended.

I chewed and I chewed and I swallered and I chewed some more. Ever eat a half-frozen steak? It ain't as easy as you might suppose. It sures make your tongue cold.

"Hank, mayday, mayday! She's . . . I'm leaving!"

I got the last bite swallered, right on schedule. I spotted the calendar on the wall and jumped up so I could read what Sally May had written on it. In the square for Monday she had written, "Beauty shop, 10:00."

Ah ha! That's why she had gone to town in such a rush. But the next square, the one for Tuesday, was the one that held the Ultimate Secret.

I started reading: "End of the . . ."

I heard the front door open. HUH? Sally May *always* went to the back door. She *never* used the front door. But she was sure as thunder using the front door this time and I was by George trapped.

CHAPTER FOUR

The Case
Is Solved

I took one last look at the calendar: "End of the month clearance sale, Stockman's Western Store."

I heard Sally May gasp in the other room. "My cactus! Who . . . what on earth . . ."

I was sitting there in the midst of the steak blood, trying to decide what to do, when she appeared in the doorway. She looked at me and her mouth dropped open. "Hank! What are you doing in here!"

I gave her a smile and started whapping my tail on the bloody floor, as if to say, "Hi Sally May, how's it going? I . . . uh . . . just got here and discovered that . . . uh . . . somebody stole your steaks, so to speak. And . . . uh . . . I realize that the . . . uh . . . evidence looks very damaging for me, but I would . . . uh . . . urge you not to leap to any . . . uh . . . hasty conclusions."

She was carrying the baby in one arm and a bag of groceries in the other. She set them down on the floor, reached into the closet, and came out with a broom. Her face was red and there were thunderclouds in her eyes.

"YOU ATE OUR LUNCH, YOU SORRY GOOD FOR NOTHING STINKING COWDOG! AND LOOK AT THIS MESS!"

How could I look at the mess when she was trying to hit me with the broom? Whap! She got me on the back. I tried to run, I mean I would have been glad to get out of her house but she had the door blocked. I ran in a circle and whap! She got me again.

So I did the only sensible thing a dog in fear of his life could do: I jumped up on the dinner table. Was it MY fault the jelly jar fell off and broke? Was it MY fault that she swung at me and hit the sugar bowl instead? I've always been the kind of dog who could take a hint. I can tell when I'm not wanted. When Sally May drew back her broom for another shot, I leaped off the table, ran between her legs, shot through the door, sprinted across the living room, and made a flying leap

through the window. And then I ran for my life.

I went down to the feed barn, figgered that would be the safest place for a dog with a price on his head. The door on the feed barn was warped at the bottom and I squeezed through and took refuge inside.

I went to the darkest corner and hid between two bales of prairie hay. After a bit I heard the pickup and stock trailer pull up to the corral. The cowboys had come in for lunch and were putting their horses in the side lot. I could hear them talking and laughing about some extraordinary roping feat they had performed that morning.

They took their roping serious, those two guys. It didn't bother them in the least that most of the sane and intelligent people in the world not only couldn't rope but didn't even want to learn. They seemed to think that if a guy could throw a rope he was something special.

I won't comment on that. I have no tacky remarks to make about grown men who walk around swinging ropes. I learned long ago not to pass judgment on others, no matter how crazy they act.

Well, the cowboys headed for the house. I could hear their spurs jingling. The back door opened and closed. Exactly one minute and thirty-two seconds later, the door opened again and I heard High Loper's voice: "Hank! Come here, you sorry devil! When I get my hands on you . . ."

I couldn't make out the last part. Wind was banging a piece of loose tin on the roof. (If I'd had any say-so in the matter, that roof would have been fixed years ago, but nobody ever listens to Hank.) Anyway, I couldn't make out the last part but I didn't really need to. Loper wasn't calling to wish me happy birthday.

He yelled for a while, then went back inside. Everything got quiet. I wondered what they were having for lunch. Whatever it was, you can be sure they didn't starve.

I mean, you've got to put all this into perspective. Loper had missed one steak dinner, right? One meal out of a whole lifetime.

Okay, then you have me, the Head of Ranch Security, who had put in years of faithful service and had eaten scraps, garbage, tasteless dry dog food, and an occasional rabbit. Wasn't I entitled to one steak dinner? Was that too much to ask for a whole lifetime?

Hence, through simple logic we discover that Sally May and Loper had ABSOLUTELY NO RIGHT TO BE MAD AT ME for eating a few crummy little steaks off their table.

Not only that but Sally May had been negligent in leaving the steaks unguarded. So there you are.

Well, the noon hour came and went. I heard the vigilantes out looking for me but I laid low and they didn't find me. Finally they went back to work. I'm sure that broke their hearts, having to do a little work for a change.

When things quieted down, I heard Drover creeping around outside. "Hank? You down here? You can come out now."

I stuck my head through the crack in the door, checked in all directions, and slithered out.

"Oh, there you are," he said. "Boy, you sure got 'em mad up at the house. What did you do this time?"

"What do you mean, 'this time'? This ain't something I do every day just for sport."

"No, I guess not. What did you do this time?"

I told him the story. "And as you can see, I was just doing my job and they've got no right to be sore at me."

"I see what you mean," said Drover. "Let's see. You knocked over the cactus. You pulled the steak dish off the table. You busted the dish. You got blood all over the kitchen. And then you ate the steaks and knocked off the jelly jar. Well . . . what was Sally May so mad about?"

"See? That's my point right there. I mean, your first reaction was the same as mine. I don't know, I just don't know. Maybe she and Loper had a fight this morning. Maybe the moon was in the wrong place."

"Maybe she was worried about the end of the world."

"Which brings us back to our investigation, Drover, and another little matter which you won't enjoy hearing about."

"Uh oh."

"That's a good way to put it." I cleared my throat. "Drover, I'm afraid I must point out that you left your post in a combat situation, ran to the machine shed, abandoned your superior when he was trapped in the house with a frenzied, dangerous, possibly crazy woman, and otherwise behaved in a disgraceful, chicken-hearted manner."

Drover looked at his feet. "Well, I was scared, Hank, and . . ."

"Spare me the details. Ordinarily this kind of cowardly behavior would have to be written up and put into your dossier. But I'm willing to forget the whole thing if you'll give me one small piece of information."

His face brightened and he started wagging his stub tail. "Sure Hank, anything you want to know, just ask me anything!"

I smiled, bent down to his ear, and whispered, "*Who* first told you that the world was going to end tomorrow at three o'clock?"

"Well, let's see." He scratched his head. "Was it you?"

"No. Think a little harder."

"Well . . . gosh, I can't remember, Hank."

"Here's a little hint: was it by any chance a cat?"

"A cat, a cat. Let's see now. You were asleep and I was up by the yard gate this morning and . . . do you reckon it could have been Pete?"

I glanced off to the east and saw Pete basking in the sun beside the garden gate. He was purring and washing himself, which means that he was spitting in his paw and wiping the spit over his face. That's the way a cat takes a bath.

I take tremendous pride in my personal appearance. I cultivate a rich, manly smell. I bathe regularly, in the sewer.

Now, let's look at Pete. He takes spit-baths. Has anyone ever seen him in the sewer? No sir. But has Sally May ever referred to him as a stinking cat? No sir. So there you are, and that's one of two dozen reasons why I hate cats and Pete in particular.

I had to get that off my chest. Now, where was I?

"Well, Drover, we've broken the case."

"You mean the world's not going to end tomorrow?"

"That's correct."

"Oh, what a relief! I tried not to show it, Hank, but I was mighty scared. But . . . are you sure we're safe?"

"I saw the calendar. It didn't say 'End of the World.' It said 'End of the month clearance sale.'"

"Oh, that's just wonderful!"

"Is it?"

"Well, maybe it's not."

"It may be good, Drover, but it's not wonderful."

"That's what I meant."

"It can't be wonderful because we were duped by the cat."

"You mean . . ."

"Yes, exactly. We broke the case but consider the price."

He cocked his head to the side. "You mean . . . at the clearance sale?"

"No, that's not what I mean, Drover, not at all. I did a flawless penetration of the house, conducted a near-perfect investigation, broke the case wide open. But my position as Head of Ranch Security has been compromised. How can I carry on my work when everyone on this ranch is mad at me?"

"Huh. I hadn't thought of that."

"Well, it's time you thought about it, son, because I have no choice but to take a leave of absence until this thing blows over."

"You mean . . ."

"Exactly. I'm leaving the ranch today and I'm liable to stay gone for a week—unless, of course, I'm offered a better position somewhere else, and then I may never come back."

"Oh. Oh. Then that means . . ."

"Exactly. You're in charge of security until I come back."

Drover's jaw dropped. "But Hank, I wouldn't live on any ranch that would have me in charge of security."

"Nor would I, but that's the way this particular cookie has crumbled. So long, Drover, I'm hitting the road. I'll see you in a couple of weeks—maybe."

"No . . . wait a minute, Hank. Where you going? What if I need some help?"

"I'm going to town to visit my sister and maybe a couple of other women. If you get into a bind, if you need any help, if there's an emergency of any kind, don't hesitate to take care of it yourself."

"But Hank . . ."

"So long, Drover, see you around."

And with that, I marched through the sick pen, through the back lot, out the corrals, and headed north toward town.

CHAPTER FIVE

A Singing Buzzard, as Incredible as That Might Seem

It was a fine afternoon for a walk. The birds were chirping, the sun was shining, a nice soft breeze was blowing, and I was walking away from all the cares and responsibilities of the ranch.

Yes, it was a wonderful afternoon for a walk. But as the hours passed, I began to realize that it wasn't such a fine afternoon for a twenty-five mile trip across the country. That's how far it was to town, and if I'd remembered how far it was, I might not have been so quick to leave the ranch.

To get to town, see, I had to pass through that rough canyon country north of headquarters. Ordinarily I could have hit a lope and made it through the rough country before dark and spent the night up on the flats, but don't forget that I had cactus spines in my feet. And that country was rough and rocky.

It slowed me down, and dadburn it, at sundown I found myself right in the middle of one of them deep canyons. And you know what that meant. This was hostile country, home of the biggest, meanest, ferociousest coyotes in Ochiltree County.

I didn't dare travel at night, so when the sun settled down on the canyon rim, I started looking for a place to hole up. In my travels and research I've discovered that one of the best places to hole up for the night is in a hole, so I started hunting for a hole.

I hadn't been looking very long when I spotted a shallow cave up on the side of a limestone cliff. That looked good to me, so I made my way up a steep incline that no ordinary dog could have climbed. I got there on sheer strength and determination.

At last I dragged myself over the rim and lay there catching my breath. Imagine my surprise when I discovered that the cave was already occupied.

I got the first clue when I heard—not voices, as you might expect, but music. Banjo music. I know that sounds strange, banjo music coming from a cave in a wild and remote canyon, but if there's anything I've learned in my years of security work, it's that this is a very strange world we live in.

And what I heard was banjo music, I don't care what you say.

Well, it had taken me fifteen minutes and a considerable investment in energy to climb up to that cave and I wasn't about to leave just because the place was occupied. I've gotten into some terrible fights over less important things.

I followed the sound of the music and crept toward the mouth of the cave. And that's when I heard the singing.

Every time I go to town,
The boys keep kicking my dog around.
Makes no difference if he is a hound.
They got to quit kicking my dog around.

Then on the chorus, the singer tried to imitate a dog howling. Well, that was enough to convince me that he wasn't a dog. No sir, it was a second-rate imitation. I mean, Hank the Cowdog will never make an opera singer, but I do know a few things about howling.

I peeked around the corner, and do you want to

guess the identity of the mysterious cave musician? Here's a few hints: big black bird, skinny neck, pot belly, ugly as twenty-three varieties of sin.

If you guessed Madame Moonshine, the witchy owl, you're wrong. If you guessed Junior the Buzzard, you win the grand prize. Yes sir, I had by George stumbled into the cliff-side home of Wallace and Junior.

I could see Junior squatting on the floor, surrounded by a bunch of rabbit bones, and he had a little old banjo on his knee. Wallace came waddling out of the back end of the cave.

"Junior! Will you quit making all that dad-ratted noise?"

"But P-P-Pa . . ."

"And here you are, a big strong boy, and I'm still having to bring home your dinner."

"But P-P-Pa . . ."

"All these years I've tried to school you."

"But P-P-Pa . . ."

"I taught you to fly. I taught you to ride the updrafts and soar in the sky. I taught you how to spot a dead rabbit on the highway, half a mile in the air."

"But P-P-Pa . . ."

"And here you are, a big strong boy, and I'm still having to bring home your dinner."

"But P-P-Pa . . ."

"Son, you're never gonna amount to Shinola as long as you play a dadgum banjo."

"B-b-but Pa, I want to b-be a s-singer when I ga-ga-grow up."

"You hush up! Don't you say that word."

"Y-you mean 's-s-singer'?"

"Yes sir, that's what I mean. It's a filthy word, and no self-respecting buzzard ever wanted to be a singer."

"P-p-pa . . . y-you said a fa-fa-fa-filthy word."

"And furthermore . . ." Just then, Wallace saw me at the mouth of the cave. "What is that?"

"What's whu-whu-whu-what, P-Pa?"

"That thang there."

Junior turned to me and grinned. "Oh b-boy, it's our d-d-doggie friend! Hi, D-D-Doggie."

"How's it going?" I said.

Old Wallace took a couple of steps toward me, stuck out his neck, and stared at me. "Is he dead? Will he eat? Son, this could be tomorrow's dinner!"

"He ain't d-dead, Pa, and he n-never has b-b-b-been."

Wallace squinted at me. "You're right, son. Go on, dog, shoo, git outa here! This here's private property!"

I walked toward the old man and showed him

some teeth. "I'm staying for the night, buzzard, and if you don't like it, I'll private *your* property."

Old Wallace shrank back. "Junior! Did you hear that? Are you gonna let a dog talk that way to your own daddy?"

"I su-su-su-suspect I w-will, Pa, cause h-he might b-b-b-bite me, bite me."

"And I guess that's more important to you than showin' respect for your own flesh and blood, your poor old daddy who's worked and slaved and scrimped and saved so's you could make something out of yourself."

"Y-y-yup, I r-r-reckon so."

The old man shook his head and went off to the back of the cave, muttering under his breath. "Well I never . . . dang kids . . . no morals, no responsibility . . . life's just one big party . . . music, bah!"

Junior looked at me and grinned. "I w-w-want to b-be a su-su-singer when I g-g-grow up, grow up, but P-Pa don't think I'll ever am-m-m-m-m, amount to anything."

"Well, I don't know about that," I said, "but you'll never go to the top with that song you were singing. You don't howl right. You're using the wrong technique. Hand me that banjo and I'll give you a few pointers on howling."

"Oh g-gosh, w-w-would you?"

He handed me the banjo and I tuned it up.

As you might suspect, buzzards have a pretty poor ear for music. The banjo was badly out of tune. I got her fine-tuned and whipped out the song.

Every time I go to town,
The boys keep kickin' my dog around.
Makes no difference if he is a hound,
They got to quit kickin' my dog around.

On the chorus I showed him how the howling should be done. Then I suggested we sing it together. On the chorus, he sang the melody with the words "Arf arf, woof woof, bark bark, bow wow," and I harmonized with one heck of a fine job of howling.

Junior was just tickled to death with our performance. "Oh g-g-gosh that was g-g-good! You s-sure know how to h-h-howl, D-Doggie."

"Well, that's one of the many things you have to do well if you're going to make a career in the security business. I guess you buzzards don't get too many opportunities to howl."

"N-n-no. P-pa never t-taught me to h-h-h-howl."

Just then I heard a howl. I looked at Junior. "Was that you?"

"N-n-no, it w-wasn't m-me."

"Well, it wasn't me either."

"And it w-w-wasn't P-Pa."

"If it wasn't me, if it wasn't you, and if it wasn't your old man, that means it wasn't any of us."

"Y-you're r-r-right."

"And that means," I lowered my voice to a whisper, "it came from someone else." We listened. There it was again. "And I think I know where it came from—a couple of drunken coyote brothers named Rip and Snort."

"Oh g-g-g-gosh, I'm s-s-s-scared of c-c-c-c-c . . . wolfs!"

"Wait right here, I'll check this out." I crept over to the ledge in front of the cave and looked down. Sure 'nuff, there sat Rip and Snort down below. "Evening, fellers, what can I do for you?"

They whispered to themselves and then Snort said, "Hunk? That you, Hunk? We hear singing, oh boy. We want sing too. We berry good to sing, have wonderful voice."

Well, I certainly didn't want to antagonize Rip and Snort, since the last time we'd met I had convinced them that the moon was made of chopped chicken liver and . . . it's too outrageous to explain. I wanted to stay on their good side.

"All right, fellers, we'll do the song again and

you boys can come in on the chorus and do your stuff. But if you want to sing with us, you've got to go by the house rules."

"Coyote not like rules. Coyote wild and happy, have berry much fun break rules, cause trouble, oh boy."

"I know that, Snort, but you can't sing with us unless you follow the rules. House rules say we've got to shut down at ten o'clock and let folks sleep. We can't carry on all night."

The brothers talked it over. Then Snort said, "Those chicken rules. Coyote not like chicken rules. But we follow."

I motioned Junior over to the ledge. He seemed a little scared but he came. "Fellers, this here's Junior. Junior, down there sits Rip and Snort, couple of buddies from my wilder days. All right boys, here we go. One, two, three, four."

I cranked up the banjo and me and Junior did the song again. Since Rip and Snort didn't know the words and weren't smart enough to learn them, they kind of grumbled along until we got to the chorus. Then they joined in.

Boy, did they howl! They cut loose and howled up a storm. It was their kind of song—no words to memorize.

If you ask me, it was a special moment in Texas

Panhandle history. I mean, the Panhandle ain't famous for its cultural achievements, but this could very well have been the by-George high point of Panhandle culture, and I'm talking about forever.

But you can't expect a buzzard to appreciate art and culture and music and such stuff, so it was no big surprise when old man Wallace came waddling out of the cave.

"What is all this noise? Junior, you quiet that racket this very minute, how can a body sleep with all that dad-ratted, ding-busted, pig-nosed, frazzlin', horrifyin' noise!"

"But P-Pa . . ."

"You put that banjo up and take yourself to bed, it's past your bedtime, you've got to get up early in the morning and go find us something dead to eat, and I don't want to hear one more word out of you tonight, GOOD NIGHT!"

Junior looked at me and shrugged, "G-g-good n-night."

"That's *two words,* Junior, and you're in deep trouble now, but go on to bed and maybe I'll forget about it." Junior waddled off to bed. The old man shot me a glare and went over to the ledge and looked down at Rip and Snort.

"Y'all have to go home now, we ain't runnin' a pool hall, go on now, scat!"

Old man Wallace might have swung some weight in the bird world but Rip and Snort didn't pay the slightest attention to him. Instead, they tuned up and started singing the only song they'd ever memorized, the Coyote Sacred Hymn and National Anthem:

Me just a worthless coyote,
Me howling at the moon.
Me like to sing and holler,
Me crazy as a loon.

Me not want job or duties,
No church or Sunday school.
Me just a worthless coyote,
And me ain't nobody's fool.

And while they sang, old Wallace was just a-fuming. "Y'all better hush up that noise and go on back where y'all came from! Now, I'm gonna get mad here and I can't be responsible for what happens! I'm a-warnin' y'all!"

You know what a buzzard does when he gets mad? I didn't know either, but I found out. *He throws up on the party that made him unhappy.*

That would be bad enough if he ate decent food. But buzzards don't eat decent food. When one throws up on you, what you're getting is dead skunks, dead rats, rot and corruption and I don't want to talk about it any more.

Let's say that Wallace expressed his feelings to Rip and Snort. Let's say that they quit singing very suddenly, even though they didn't want to. Let's say that they got the heck out of there and it became very still outside.

Then Wallace looked at me. "How 'bout you, pup?"

"I was just fixing to turn in, sir. I'm awful sleepy."

Wallace burped and went back into the cave, grumbling to himself. "Danged drunks . . . guy can't get a night's sleep anymore . . . coyotes thinking they can carry on all night . . . huh!"

CHAPTER SIX

A Happy Reunion
with My Sister

The next morning I awoke to the sound of birds.

"Junior, git yourself outa that bed! It's morning and we're burnin' daylight."

"But P-Pa, I'm t-t-tired."

"Well you ought to be, stayin' up half the night. And *you,* dog . . ." I opened my eyes and looked into a face so ugly that it could have come straight out of a nightmare. ". . . and *you,* dog, it's time for you to go on home. We ain't takin' you to raise."

My first and most natural instinct was to growl at something that awful looking, and then maybe to attack. But I caught myself just as the growl was building in my throat. I remembered how Wallace had got rid of Rip and Snort the night before. I didn't think I could stand that, first thing in the morning.

"Yes sir," I said, "matter of fact I was just fixing to leave. Adios Junior, see you around." In a flash, I was out of the cave.

"B-b-bye D-Doggie," Junior waved his wing.

Wallace followed me out. "One of these days maybe we'll have you for supper."

I didn't wait around to find out how he meant that. I vamoosed, found a cow trail that led out of the canyon, and headed for town.

If you ever have a chance to wake up and see a buzzard first thing in the morning, you'll want to avoid it. That's what you call a rude awakening.

Once I had climbed out of the canyon and hit the rolling prairie country to the north, I had smooth traveling all the way to town. I reached the city limits about one o'clock that afternoon and traveled down alleys until I found the place where my sister stayed.

Hadn't seen the gal in a couple of years and I was kind of looking forward to the reunion.

She stayed around an old two story house on the south edge of town, had a big backyard and several vacant lots around it. If a guy had to live in town, it wasn't a bad place.

The back gate was shut and a lot of dogs would

have turned around right there and gone back home, but a locked gate never meant much to me. All you need is powerful back legs and remarkable athletic ability and you can hop over any gate that's ever been built.

I cleared that rascal with six inches to spare. I mean, you'd have thought I was a deer the way I soared over it. Didn't see the tricycle on the other side until it was too late. Kind of banged me up when I lit in the middle of it. Got a handlebar right on the end of my nose.

I made a pass around the yard and sniffed out the whole situation—trees, shrubs, posts, flower-beds, tool shed, lawn chairs, barbecue grill, the whole deal. This was a habit I'd built up after years and years of dealing with outlaws, wild animals, and dangerous characters. A guy never knows what he's getting into until he knows what he's getting into.

My motto has always been, "Don't take anything for granite because that's what tombstones are made of."

Anyway, I sniffed out the entire yard and left my signature on a couple of shrubs and a clothesline pole, just to serve notice on the local mutts that criminal activity was liable to be dangerous for a few days.

As I was signing the clothesline pole, I noticed something odd. There was a houseshoe on the bottom of it, you know, a kind of slipper. Well, that was one of the strangest things I'd ever seen. I mean, I know I'm country and not in touch with your latest trends and fashions in town, but still . . .

Why would anybody put a *houseshoe* at the base of a clothesline pole? There was something peculiar going on around that place, and I figgered that after I signed the pole I'd better conduct a more thorough investigation.

I mean, my sister was living in that yard, and I've always been kind of protective of my sis.

All of a sudden I heard a scream. This next part will be hard for a lot of people to believe, so before I go any further I'll need to establish my credibility as a witness. My years of security work have trained me to be a keen observer and a thorough investigator. I never exaggerate the facts and I'm not easily fooled.

In other words, I'm putting all my reputation behind this next part. I swear it's the whole truth and nothing but the truth. You can take it or leave it.

Okay, here's what happened. As I was putting my signature on the clothesline pole, *it turned into a human leg.* The leg was attached to a woman and it was she who let out the scream. I was stunned by the scream, don't you see, well, you can imagine what a shocker that was, a clothesline pole turning into a woman.

Just for a second I stared at her and she stared at me. Then she hit me over the head with a clothespin bag and squalled: "Get out of my yard, you nasty dog!"

She swung at me again. No ordinary dog could have dodged that second shot. I did but it was nothing in the world but exceptional athletic ability that saved me. And then I made a dash for the fence.

Out of the corner of my eye I saw Maggie— that's my sister—saw Maggie coming out of her doghouse. "Henry, is that you?"

"Hi Mag, how's it going, yeah I . . ." A rock zinged past my ear. ". . . check you later, Sis." I vaulted the fence and took cover in some weeds.

I stayed hid for half an hour, figgered that would give events enough time to settle down, then I went back to the fence. But this time I took no chances. Before I jumped back into the yard, I checked things out through a knothole. I wanted to be derned sure that neither of those clothesline poles was wearing a slipper.

I hopped the fence again and sneaked over to the doghouse. Mag was out front, sunning herself in the . . . well, in the sun. She saw me coming and walked out to meet me.

"Well, Henry, it's been a long time." All at once she wrinkled her nose and backed away. "What's that horrible smell?"

I froze. "Don't move, Maggie, let me check it out. It could be something serious." I lifted my nose and took an air sample. "Okay, relax, I don't smell a thing."

"You don't smell *that*?"

"What? No, I did a test and it checked out negative. I don't smell a thing."

She lifted her nose and sniffed the air. She took two steps toward me, sniffed, and coughed. "Oh, it's only you."

"What do you mean, it's only me? What did you expect?"

"The odor, Henry. You smell a little ranchy."

"Oh."

"What a wonderful surprise, Henry. Uh, what was your difficulty with Mrs. Gregg?"

"Who?"

"Mrs. Gregg, the mistress of the house, our dear friend and benefactor, the wonderful lady who chased you out of the yard half an hour ago."

"Oh, her. Say, that was a crazy deal." I told her about how the clothesline pole had turned into a woman.

She rolled her eyes. "Oh Henry, how could you be so crude! Oh, I'm so glad the children weren't . . ."

"Too bad the kids weren't here to see that. What a story! I'll be sure to tell 'em about it. Say, where are the kids?"

"They've gone to obedience school. They'll not be back until late, and they'll be so sorry they missed you."

I went over and flopped down in front of the doghouse. "Well heck, I can stick around for a while. As a matter of fact . . ."

Maggie rushed over to me. "Oh no, Henry, we understand how busy you must be. We mustn't be greedy with your time, I mean we understand that a dog with a position as important as yours . . ."

"It is an important position, Mag. I mean, just stop and think about one dog running a six thousand acre ranch all by himself. It's a twenty-four hour a day job, and danger is never far away."

"Indeed, and it would be irresponsible for us to keep you away from your work. No, we just couldn't ask you to stay, as much as we would like to."

"Well, if it really means that much to you . . ."

"It does, Henry, it really does, but I do understand . . .

". . . I could probably stick around for a couple of days."

"Of course there will be other times, won't there? And we mustn't grieve, must we?"

She smiled at me and I smiled at her. "No, we mustn't grieve, Maggie."

"No indeed."

"Life's just too short for that."

"Yes it is."

"Let's leave grief to the grievers."

"Well put, Henry. I'm so sorry."

"And so am I." We hugged each other. "I'll stay, but only for a couple of days and only because it means so much to you and the kids."

Her smile wilted. She stared at me with wide eyes, and then a strange thing happened. She placed a paw over her forehead and rolled over on her back. And she moaned.

I rushed to her side. "Maggie, what is it, speak to me, I'm right here at your side!"

She opened her eyes. "It's these headaches. Nerves, tension, too much company. I just need to be absolutely still for two days and it'll go away. Maybe it would be better if you came back another time, Henry."

"And leave my sister alone on death's door? A lot of dogs would do that, just walk away from hard times, but you've got a different kind of brother."

"Yes, I know."

"And if I have to stay here a whole month, I'll see you through this crisis!"

"Oh my heavens!"

Just then we heard a bunch of little feet on the sidewalk, and a little voice called out, "Hi Mom, we're back!" I looked around and saw my nieces and nephews, four of the cutest little cowdog pups that was ever built.

When they saw me there beside their ma, they stopped and stared. Then Roscoe, one of the boys, cried out, "It's Uncle Hank! Oh boy! Hi, Uncle Hank, can you stay the night?" They came at a run and swarmed all over me, licked me on the face and all that stuff.

"Will you tell us a story, Uncle Hank?" asked Spot, the other boy. "Please?"

I turned to my sis. "Well Mag, I guess that settles it. I really should get back to the ranch, but dadgone it, a guy just can't walk away and disappoint these kids. I guess I can stay a couple of days."

The kids cheered. Maggie covered her eyes with a paw.

"How's the headache, Sis?"

"I think it's just beginning," she said.

CHAPTER SEVEN

Garbage Patrol

Me and Maggie was both ranch-raised but we went in different directions when we reached maturity. I stuck with the ranch life and went into full-time security work, and she moved to town.

For some reason she never took to ranch life. Growing up, it seemed that everything we pups did was either too loud or too dirty for her. Just to give you an example, we never could get her to go into the sewer with us. She just didn't take to it.

She never cared a lick about chewing on smelly old bones either, or playing in the mud or digging holes. She didn't even have an interest in cow work.

Moving into town was a good thing for her.

She found a good home and staked out her own version of cowdog life, which always seemed a little strange to me but I wouldn't want to judge anybody else.

Oh, and she never went in for nicknames either. The blessed woman will go to her grave calling herself Margaret and me Henry. She always thought Hank sounded undignified or something like that.

But even though me and Sis went our different ways, we remained close over the years, and she was always delighted when I dropped in for a visit. She kind of looked up to me as her big brother, see, and I think it kind of tickled her for me to drop in and talk to the kids about the old cowdog ways—you know, show 'em how country dogs lived and tell 'em some stories, that kind of thing.

Oh, every now and then she'd put on like she didn't want her young'uns exposed to such crude ways, but I knew that down deep, where it really counted, she was glad to have me there with the kids. Who wouldn't be? It ain't every town kid that has an uncle who runs a six thousand acre ranch and fights . . . I guess I've already mentioned that. Anyway, her kids were pretty lucky.

Well, poor old Mag had that headache problem and had to go to bed with it. I stuck my head in the doghouse door and told her not to worry about the kids, I would take care of everything. She let out a groan. I guess that old head was really throbbing.

Well, I went out and called the children in from their play. "All right, kids, let me have your attention for a minute or two. Your ma has asked me . . ."

Little April, one of the girls, held up her paw. "Uncle Hank, Mom doesn't allow us to call her 'Ma.' She says it sounds crude and backward. She says only dog trash uses that word."

"I see. Well, by George if that's what Mom says, that's the way it'll be. Your Mom has asked me to teach you little rascals a dab or two about your cowdog heritage."

Roscoe stared at me with big eyes. "OUR MOTHER said that? Cowdog heritage?"

"That's right, son, those were her very words, as I recall. I spoke with her only moments ago."

"Wow! We thought she was ashamed of her family."

I reached down and patted the lad on the head. "My boy, your ma . . . mother . . . mom, whatever she is, has always looked back on her cowdog heritage with enormous pride, and of course we all know what she thinks of your Uncle Hank."

Four pairs of eyes stared up at me. It got very quiet.

"Anyway, at your mother's request, I'm going to give you kids a few lessons in Cowdogology. I want you to pay attention and follow directions. Any questions?" One paw went up.

"Yes."

It was Barbara, the other girl. "What does 'ignert jackass of an uncle' mean?"

I pondered that. "A donkey is a four-legged beast of burden, sometimes referred to as a jackass. If a guy had an uncle who was a donkey, he might refer to the uncle in that way. Any more questions?" The same little girl raised her paw. "Yes?"

"Are we kin to any donkeys?"

I got a chuckle out of that. It's amazing how town kids really don't understand basic concepts of biology. "No, sweetie, it's not possible. All right, our first lesson will be, how to dig under the yard fence." The kids looked kind of shocked. "What's the matter?"

"Mom said we should never *ever* dig under the fence," said Barbara.

"That's exactly right, honey, unless Uncle Hank's here to supervise. Everybody ready? Form a line and let's move out."

We marched across the yard in single file. "Left, left, left right left! Left, left, left right left! Straighten up that line! Pick up your paws! Stick them tails up in the air! That's better. Left, left, left right left! Column . . . halt!"

They came to a halt in front of the fence and stood at attention. I walked down the line. "All right, I need four volunteers to dig a hole under the fence. You four right there. Stand by to dig . . . commence digging!"

Let me tell you, for a bunch of little town pups they did all right. There for a while the dirt was just fogging and it didn't take them long to get a tunnel dug. Then I gave the order to commence burrowing. One by one, the kids dived into the hole and wiggled through to the other side.

I served as rear outlook while they went through, then I dived into the hole and joined them on the other side.

"All right, that was pretty good. I'm glad to see that we have some spirit in this outfit, some of that good old cowdog spizzerinctum. Now we'll have a lesson on how to live off the land. We're going to make a garbage patrol."

I paced back and forth in front of them. "Suppose you were in a strange town. You didn't know anyone, you didn't have a place to stay, you didn't know where your next meal was coming from. What would you do? Form a line and follow me. I'll show you."

We marched down the alley until we came to the first garbage can, which was a fifty-five gallon drum with the top cut out. I showed 'em how to go up on their hind legs, hook their paws over the edge of the barrel, and pull it over.

"All right, now you kids sort through that stuff and find some grub." The boys gave a yell and went into the barrel, but the girls kind of hung back. "What's the matter?"

April spoke up. "Mom says that playing in garbage is unladylike."

Barbara nodded. "And we're not supposed to get dirty. Mom said so."

"Well, moms are always right, don't forget that," I said. "So go through that garbage in a ladylike manner and try not to get dirty. And don't worry about your mom. I'll take care of her."

The girls looked at each other, grinned, and dived into the barrel with the boys.

They didn't find much in that first barrel, just a couple of chicken bones and a whole bunch of newspapers, so we moved on to the next one. Same story there: corn cobs and potato peelings. By George, that was kind of a lean alley. We had to investigate a dozen barrels before we found a real treasure: a bunch of fish heads wrapped in newspaper.

Oh, the kids loved them fish heads! They jumped right in the middle of them and gobbled them down. I stood back and watched and, you know, kind of remembered myself at that age, when all at once a man stepped out into the alley. Guess he was dumping trash or something.

He looked up and down the alley. You might say we'd left a little mess. I mean, when you get all caught up in a garbage patrol, you don't stop to think about the mess you're making.

The man dropped his trash basket and came running toward us, yelling and waving his arms. "Hyah! Get outa here, go on!"

I sounded the retreat and we lit a shuck, headed south down the alley as fast as we could go. We went several blocks and hid in a hedge row. The kids were out of breath and all excited.

"Gosh, that was fun!" said Roscoe, and the others agreed.

"I was scared," said Barbara. "I thought that old man would catch us."

"Yeah," said April, "he sure looked mean!"

"Uncle Hank," said Spot, "I like fish heads."

"And playing in garbage is fun!" said Barbara.

I smiled and nodded my head. "You see, kids? If we hadn't gone on a garbage patrol, you never would have learned all this. As your mom's told you many times, education is very important."

I stepped out of the hedge and scouted the area to make sure the coast was clear, then I gave the password—"Stinkeroo," was the secret word—and the kids formed a line and we went marching home. I figgered they'd had enough education for one day.

We were marching down the alley, maybe three blocks from home, when we passed a yard with a big cedar fence around it. Sitting on top of the fence was a big fat yellow cat.

My ears shot up and my lip curled, all on sheer instinct. I mean, my instincts about cats are pretty sharp. I glared at her as we went trooping by, just waiting for her to make some kind of smart remark.

You know my position on cats. I don't like 'em. I don't go out of my way to cause trouble with a cat, but any time I find one that's shopping around for a fight, I can usually be talked into it.

Well, this cat looked dumber than most but she must have had a little bit of sense because she didn't say a word as we went past. She just stared at us.

I supposed that was the end of it, but when we got past her, little Roscoe came trotting up to the front of the column. He had a worried expression on his face.

"Uncle Hank, that cat said something when we went past."

"Hold it! Halt!" The column came to a halt. "What was that again? The cat *said something*? What exactly did the cat say?"

"She said, 'Your momma wears combat boots.' What does that mean, Uncle Hank?"

"What that means, young feller, is that we're fixing to have a demonstration of violence and bloodshed. About face! Follow me!"

And we marched back to teach some manners to a certain lard-tailed yellow cat.

CHAPTER EIGHT

The
Big Showdown

If there's anything I can't stand, it's an insolent cat. This one was insolent. I could see it on her face—that snotty self-righteous, self-satisfied smirk that just drives me nuts.

I marched up to the fence. She was sprawled out on the top board, maybe five feet above the ground.

"I understand you made some smart remark about the mother of these children. Maybe I should point out a couple of things to you. Number one, their mother is a wonderful woman. Number two, she's very sick today. Number three, she happens to be my sister. Number four, I don't like cats. And number five, if you don't take back your smart remark, you could be in very serious trouble."

She yawned. "Wait just a minute, would you?"

She leaned over the other side of the fence and called someone. Three homely little kittens crawled up beside her. "I want the kids to hear this. Children, these are dogs. Remember our little talk about dogs? The ugly one is full-grown and the others are pups. I want you to pay close attention." She turned back to me. "Would you repeat what you just said, all that number one, number two stuff?"

"You bet. Your little urchins might learn something." I repeated it. "And number five, if you don't take back your smart remark, you could be in very serious trouble."

The cat turned to her children. "I said their momma wears combat boots." The kittens laughed and squealed. "And the Big Yukk didn't like it." They laughed some more. "And Big Yukk wants to make something of it." Oh, they thought that hilarious.

"You got that right, sister. I'll try to keep control of my temper, but if you keep talking trash like that, I can't be responsible for my actions."

The old bag turned to her kids again. "Now children, remember what I said about dogs, how they're not very smart? Here is a perfect example. As long as we're on the fence and he's on the ground, we can do and say anything we wish."

I turned to my bunch. "Kids, we might as well add this to your education, so study your lessons and pay attention. Here we have a dumb cat teaching her kittens how to be dumb. The old lady thinks she's safe on that fence, which means she's never dealt with cowdogs before."

"You see the shape of the head?" the mother cat went on. "You'll notice how crude it is. That's a mark of the breed."

"It's common knowledge," I went on, "that tearing down entire fences, even stout ones, is just part of a day's work for a cowdog. I mean, reducing a fence like that one to a pile of splinters is nothing special to your Uncle Hank."

"And you'll notice," the cat said, "how dogs like to brag and boast."

"You'll notice, kids, that you very seldom get anywhere talking to a cat. They've got a smart-alecky streak that begins at the base of the skull and runs all the way to the tail."

"And now, children, we'll have an exercise in dog pesteration."

"And now, kids, we'll give Big Momma one last chance to repent." I turned to the old lady. "You want to take back what you said about my sister and the mother of these lovely children?"

"Kittens, sing along with me, to the tune of 'America the Beautiful.' Ready, two, three,"

Your momma wears old tow-sack drawers,
And hold them up with twine.
She has a ringworm on her nose
And picks it all the time.
Your momma's combat boots smell bad,
So do her dirty socks.
Which goes to show what all cats know:
All dogs are just a pox.

When they finished the song, all four cats looked down at us and grinned. And I might point out that they had terrible voices.

"Uncle Hank," said Barbara, "they're making fun of our momma and I don't like it!"

"I know, hun, I heard the whole thing."

Little Roscoe came up, and he looked mad. "What are we going to do, Uncle Hank? We can't let 'em get by with that."

"You're right, son. All right, pups, let's have a meeting of the War Council." We huddled up and made some medicine. I asked which of the kids could sing. Turned out that April and Barbara had terrific voices and the boys were, well, tolerable good.

We came up with a plan of action and turned back to the cats. They were still grinning. "All right, pups, let 'em have it." We bombarded them cats with a song of our own, to the tune of "My Bonnie Lies Over the Ocean." I stationed April and Barbara on the front line:

When God made a cat He was desperate
For something to make Himself laugh.
He gave it the brain of a monkey
But dropped it and broke it in half.

Cats are stoo-pid,
They don't have the sense of a snooker ball.
That's why monkeys
Deny any kinship at all.

"Nice work, pups!" I said. "Let's do that chorus again, but this time with harmony and passion. Lead off, April! Sock it to 'em Barbara!"

We gave them cats another dose of the chorus, and it was just by George wonderful. When we finished, the cats weren't laughing or grinning anymore. Big Momma had a sour look on her face.

"That was the worst singing I ever heard," she yowled. "Kittens, that was a typical performance from a group of low-class, poorly bred garbage dogs."

"Garbage dogs! Now wait a minute . . ."

"The dog that eats garbage thinks garbage. That's one of the laws of science."

"You're fixing to learn some other laws of science if you don't watch your mouth."

"They're crude, rude, uncouth, and socially unacceptable."

"And about half-dangerous, you forgot that one."

"And since they have no talent, no poetic gifts, no subtlety, no reasoning faculty, what they do best is BARK."

"Oh yeah?"

She wrinkled her nose at me. "Yeah."

"*Oh yeah?*"

"*Yeah!*"

"Well I got news for you lady. There's more talent in one of these cowdog pups than in a whole trainload of cats."

"Very well," she said, "we'll just see about that." She turned to her urchins. "All right, kittens, on the count of three, we shall hiss. One, two, three!" They all humped up their backs and started hissing.

"Okay, that does it! Pups, this is war. Diplomacy is wasted on a bunch of alley cats. Form a line and

stand by for growling!" The kids got into position and waited for the command. "Ready on the left? Ready on the right? Aim . . . growl!"

We let 'em have it, some of the best growling I'd ever heard. The kids did a terrific job and I was proud to be there.

Old momma cat didn't like that even a little bit. "All right, kittens, you've heard the enemy. As you can see, he's big, dumb, and loud. On the count of three, we'll answer with yowling and second degree hissing. One, two, three!"

They humped up, yowled, and hissed at us.

"Pups," I called out, "stand by to bark! By George, if it's war they want, it's war they'll get. And remember the cowdog motto: 'Do unto others but don't take trash off the cats.' Ready on the left? Ready on the right? Aim . . . BARK!"

Boy, you never heard such barking. Them kids just raptured the air . . . ruptured the air, whatever . . . just set up a thunderous barrage of barking. It was a nice piece of work.

Old lady cat was getting madder and madder. "Very well, kittens, we shall have to give them the maximum load. On the count of three, give them yowling, third degree hissing, and SPITTING! One, two, three!"

All four of the little dunces leaned over the fence and let 'er rip. Ordinarily I can control myself in the face of yowling and hissing, even third degree hissing. But hey, that spitting . . . no sir. No cat spits at Hank the Cowdog and lives to spit another day.

"All right, pups, they've pushed us to the limit! This is all-out war. Prepare to attack the fence and don't bother to take prisoners! Ready on the left!

Ready on the right! Take aim . . . attack, charge, bonzai!"

Barking at the top of our lungs, we launched the first wave against the fence, with the cats hissing and spitting at us from the top. Oh, it was a battle to remember!

The fence was made of solid wood, don't you see, and I had calculated that it would take two or three waves for us to lay it flat on the ground. It was our rotten luck that several people in the neighborhood came out their back doors to see what all the noise was about.

A big guy in a T-shirt came fogging out of the house that belonged to the fence we were in the process of destroying. "Joan, call the dog pound," he yelled, "we got a pack of stray dogs back here! Hyah, git outa here, you dadgum barking fools!"

When I saw him coming and heard him mention the dog pound, I canceled the invasion and sounded the retreat. "To the house, pups, run as fast as you can, retreat!"

They peeled off and headed north down the alley as fast as their little legs would take them. I waited until the last pup had made his escape and then I looked up at the cats.

"We'll meet again, cat, and when we do that fence won't be worth the paper it's printed on."

Don't know why I said it that way. If you think about it, it don't make a lot of sense, I mean, fences aren't exactly . . . in the heat of battle a guy sometimes . . . never mind.

The old hag had a big grin on her face, looked so smug and self-satisfied I was tempted to risk capture and death just to clean her off that fence and teach her some manners.

"I told you we could make you bark," she said.

"Yeah, and don't you ever forget it!"

Just then, that maniac in the T-shirt reached the back gate and filled the air with rocks and sticks. "Git outa here, you sorry flea-bitten mutt! Go on, leave my cats alone!"

So there you are. The entire incident had started when one of his precious cats had made a vicious, scandalous remark about my sister, the mother of my nieces and nephews. When will the human race learn that cats create 83% of all the trouble in the world and start 93% of all the fights?

I mean, statistics don't lie. I pulled these statistics out of the hat, so to speak, and while they may not be 100% accurate, they don't lie. Yet the human race continues to rush to the defense of . . . oh well. There's no use getting upset just because the world is all wrong and I happen to be right 96% of the time.

I ran from the scene, and with my amazing speed I reached the tunnel just as the last pup was crawling back into the yard. It was none too soon. At the end of the block, I saw a white pickup with a wire cage in the back.

Painted on the door was a big police badge, along with the words, CITY OF TWITCHELL DOGCATCHER.

CHAPTER NINE

The Mysterious Ivory Dog Bar

I dived into the tunnel and wiggled my way through to the other side. Then I held my breath and listened. The pickup came down the alley. It slowed, then sped up and kept going.

I had dodged another bullet. My sister wouldn't have been too proud of me if I had got her kids throwed in the dog pound.

The pups came running up to me, jumping up and down, yipping, licking me on the face, you know how pups do. They were all excited.

"Oh boy, Uncle Hank," said Roscoe, "that was the funnest thing we've ever done!"

"Yeah," said Spot, "we like being cowdogs. I can't wait to tell Mom!"

"Hey, wait a minute, hold it right there, son," I

said. "Something tells me we'd best keep our adventures to ourselves. Your ma might take a dim view of it. Mum's the word, kids."

They all grinned and nodded, and for the next fifteen minutes they went around whispering "Mum's the word" to each other.

Not long after we got back, Maggie came out of the doghouse. Said she'd had a nice long nap and her head was feeling some better. She asked what we'd done while she was asleep, and I said, "Oh, nothing much. We had a little snack and did some singing."

She stared at me and kind of twisted her head to the side. "Really? Singing? Well, I must say that surprises me."

I must say she'd have been even more surprised if she'd known where and how and why we'd done our singing, but what she didn't know wasn't hurting her.

"You've got some very talented children," I said. "Yes sir, they sure do a good job of singing, especially them gals."

"Well thank you, Henry. I confess . . . well, I just didn't think you cared about culture and refinement. Maybe I've underestimated you."

"It's entirely possible, Mag, I mean, just because I've been trained to be a dangerous

85

weapon doesn't mean I can't appreciate beautiful music and poetry and that other stuff."

The kids were pretty well tuckered out after our garbage patrol and the cat episode, and they stretched out in the yard and took naps in the sun. But every now and then April and Barbara would sit up and go to scratching. Maggie noticed, and about the third time it happened, she went over to check it out.

"Barbara, what are you doing? April, why are you scratching? You know that's not ladylike."

For some reason the girls looked at me. "Oh nothing, Mom," said April. "We just . . ."

Maggie moved closer, squinted her eyes, and studied Barbara's hair. She gasped, *"Fleas!"* Then April started scratching her ear. "You too! What . . . where . . ."

For some reason she looked in my direction. Why was everybody staring at me? I mean, anyone can catch fleas from a bunch of scroungy cats, but is that my fault?

Mag turned back to Barbara. "And furthermore, young lady, you smell like dead fish! What on earth have you girls been doing?"

Well, they started crying. I guess they'd never had fleas before and thought it was something horrible. I couldn't hear all that was being said over there, but I had a suspicion that my nieces were spilling the beans. And I had another suspicion that a storm was fixing to strike Uncle Hank.

Maggie gave the kids a severe lecture and sent 'em to bed in the middle of the afternoon. Then she came over to where I was uh, countin' my change, you might say, and trying to look as innocent as possible.

"Listen, Maggie, let me explain. I just thought . . ."

"No, it's all right Henry. I understand."

"You do?"

She gave me a sweet smile, which sort of surprised me. "The children talked you into taking them on a little romp."

"Well . . ."

"And you were too nice to say no."

"Well, yes but . . ."

"And you told them to stay out of the garbage and to leave the cats alone but they didn't."

"No, they didn't, Maggie."

"And so they've come home stinking and covered with fleas, which is just what they deserve."

"Well, Mag, I didn't want to . . . I mean, they're awful sweet kids . . ."

"But kids will be kids."

"Right, they sure will, but I hope you're not . . ."

"Mad at you? Why Henry, how could I be mad at *you*?"

"I see what you mean, Mag. You're right. How could you be mad at me?"

Heh, heh, I'd dodged another bullet. I kind of hated for the kids to catch all the blame, but what the heck, they were young, they would survive.

Well, Mag asked if I was hungry yet and I said yes, as a matter of fact I was. She said that was great because she had a special meal for me. "And now that the children are out of the way, we can have a quiet meal and talk about old times."

As you can imagine, I was delighted to see Maggie in such good spirits. She brought me some supper. Said it was a new kind of dog food and she'd been saving it for a special occasion.

It sure looked odd to me—well, I shouldn't say "odd" because that sounds too critical, and I'd be the last guy on this earth to criticize his sister's grub. It was different.

Where your ordinary run of dog food is brown and shaped in kernels or biscuits, this stuff was pure white and shaped in a rectangle—more of a bar than a biscuit, don't you see. Had a different smell too. Where your Co-op dog food will have the smell of stale grease, this new brand had kind of a perfumey smell.

Mag brought a real pretty red dog bowl and set it in front of me, and then she dropped the bar of dog food into the bowl. It hit with a clunk.

"Hey, that looks great, Sis."

"I think you'll like it, Henry."

"Sis, nobody rustles grub like you. I mean, food just seems to taste better at your place. Uh, what do you call this recipe?"

"There's the name right there." She pointed to the bar, and sure enough it had a name on it.

"Huh, I-v-o-r-y. Ivory, is that it?"

"Uh-huh. Ivory Dog Bars. The children just *adore* them."

"Well by George, if my nieces and nephews say they're good, they're bound to be good. How do you eat this thing? I mean, when a guy's in town, he wants to do things proper."

"Yes, one does. Oh, just bite off a piece and," she started giggling, "chew it up."

"Sis, I can't tell you how glad I am to see you laughing again. I mean, that headache business really had me worried. It makes the whole trip worthwhile, just seeing you laugh."

"Thank you, Henry, it's nice of you to," she started laughing again, "say so."

"Yeah, it's great. You know, it kind of reminds me of the time me and you were down by the septic tank—chasing a butterfly, as I recall. You remember that?"

"I sure do Henry. The butterfly landed on a weed out in that nasty green water."

"And you leaned out over the water . . ."

"Yes, yes, and you pushed me in!" she laughed.

I laughed. "Sure as heck did. Boy, did you hate that! And do you remember how we laughed about it?"

"Uh, go on with your supper, Henry. Yes, I sure do."

"Yeah, we just . . ." I took a big bite out of the dog bar and started chewing it up. Say, that stuff had a strange taste. Real strange, nothing at all like Co-op.

Sis was watching me. "How do you like it?"

"Huh? Oh, the dog bar? Hey, it's super, Mag, it's really . . ." I swallered the first bite. ". . . out of this world."

That pleased her. "I'm so glad you like it. I would have been crushed if you hadn't."

"Right, no it's . . . it's a little different, Mag, but you know me, I'm always anxious to try something . . . different."

"How sweet! Well, take another bite and go on

with your story."

I bit off another hunk. "Well, there you were in the sewer, up to your brisket, and . . ." I could hardly believe my eyes. A big bubble came out of my mouth. It grew and grew, and then it popped.

Mag was staring at me. "Is anything wrong?"

"Did you see that?"

"See what?"

"That great big bubble that came out of my mouth?"

She laughed. "Oh Henry, you're such a tease! Just for a moment I thought you were serious."

"Did you really?" Just for a moment, I'd thought I was serious too. Matter of fact, I could have sworn I saw a big bubble.

"How's the Ivory Dog Bar?"

"Oh Sis, this stuff is just . . . I swallered the bite I had in my mouth. "This stuff is really . . ." I burped. I mean, it just snuck out, I couldn't stop it.

"Hen-reeeeee!"

"Excuse me, Maggie, that's terrible manners."

"It really is. Oh well, I suppose that's just your way of showing how much you enjoy the meal."

"It is, it sure is, and thanks for being so . . ." There was another bubble coming out of my mouth. It popped. "Did you see that?"

She leaned over and patted me on the cheek.

"You big old teaser, you can't fool me with that again. Now go on and eat and finish your story."

To be truthful about it, I didn't want to go on and eat. I mean, I could have quit right there and been satisfied. But she was sitting in front of me and I sure as heck didn't want her to think . . . I took another bite.

"Anyway, there you were out there in the water and we got to laughing . . ."

"Yes, I remember," she said. "But you know, it's odd that I don't remember it the same way you do. I have a very clear recollection of *you* laughing, while I stood in the water and cried. Now isn't that . . . Henry? What is that on your mouth?"

"Huh?" I wiped a paw across my mouth and looked at it. "Looks kind of like foam, don't it? By George, I believe it is foam."

"Foam!" Her eyes widened. "Henry, *you're foaming at the mouth*! You don't like my supper!"

"Now Mag . . ."

"You weren't telling the truth, you hate my cooking, you always have, oh I'm a complete failure!"

"Hey listen, Mag, that foam don't mean a thing, shucks I foam at the mouth all the time."

"Lies, lies! You *hate* my cooking!"

"No, Mag, I love it, honest."

She looked at me through tear-filled eyes. "Then why haven't you finished the Ivory Dog Bar?"

"Because . . . well . . . here it goes, down the old hatch." I took the rest of the bar in my mouth, chewed it up, and swallered the heck out of it. "There you see, Sis, and you thought I didn't like . . ."

All at once I felt sick, and I mean SICK. My mouth foamed and dripped and drooled, and I could have sworn that I saw some more of them

bubbles.

"What were you saying?"

My head started to swim. I looked at Mag and thought I might toss my cookies right there. "I was . . . saying . . . how delicious . . . what do you reckon they put . . . in them dog bars, 'cause boy, they sure are good."

"Oh Henry, do you really mean that? You really liked it? Oh, I'm so thrilled! I'll serve it for breakfast tomorrow."

"S'wunnerful, Mag, just wunnerful, mercy, I got to go check on . . . excuse me a minute."

I didn't want to get sick in front of my sister, so I made a dash for the alley, by way of the tunnel we had dug under the fence.

I made it just in time. Out in the alley I had to pitch my cookies. What came up was bubbles, hundreds of 'em, thousands of 'em, green 'uns, red 'uns, pink 'uns, more bubbles than I'd ever seen in my whole life.

I was sitting there, contemplating all those bubbles, when I heard a pickup coming down the alley. It went past, screeched to a stop, and backed up. It was a white pickup with a wire cage in back.

The man inside stared at me, then got on his two-way radio. "Mobile 13 to city hall. Larry,

94

this is Jimmy Joe. I've got a code three, man, a rabid dog in the alley behind the Gregg's house. He's foaming at the mouth, Larry, send me some help!"

I glanced around. I hadn't seen any rabid dog. In fact, it appeared to me that I was the only dog in the . . .

HUH?

That guy thought I had rabies!

CHAPTER TEN

On Death Row

That guy was the dogcatcher, see, and when he got out of his pickup and started creeping toward me with a butterfly net, I began to suspect that I was in the wrong place at the wrong time.

"Hold still, doggie," he said. "Just two more steps and I'll take you for a little ride."

Who did he think he was talking to? I mean, how dumb would you have to be to fall for that "hold still doggie" business? I showed him a few fangs and gave him a growl, and fellers, he dropped that butterfly net and flew back into the pickup.

"Mobile three to city hall! Larry, he attacked me, almost got my leg, for gosh sakes send some police and the ambulance, this mutt has hydrophobia, I ain't kidding!"

It occurred to me that I had better make a run for the high and lonesome. I could have gone back into the yard, but I didn't want to cause trouble for Maggie, not after she'd been so nice and fixed me the special supper.

I headed south down the alley. I was still feeling a little weak, don't you see, and my back end didn't follow my front end. By this time the dogcatcher was perched on the cab of his pickup, talking on the radio.

"Mobile three to city hall. Suspect is proceeding south and holy cow, Larry, he's got the blind staggers, better tell 'em to seal off the whole south end of town, Larry, I mean he's out of his head and extremely dangerous!"

I could hear the sirens now, three or four of 'em moving down Main Street. I started running. The derned bubbles were still coming out of my mouth.

What the heck had brought on all the bubbles? I'd had indigestion before, ate some aged mutton with a bunch of coyotes one time and it sure made me sick, but I'd never made bubbles or foamed at the mouth.

I looked up ahead and saw a police car in the alley, so I veered off to the left and started across a vacant lot but there was a fire truck coming straight at me. I wheeled around and ran back to the alley, figgered I'd leap over a fence and vanish in somebody's backyard, but my leaper was out of commission. Too weak in the knees.

I was trapped against the fence, surrounded by police with guns and firemen with axes and the dogcatcher with his net. They were closing in on me.

I heard a sound on the fence above me. I looked around and saw that same fat yellow cat and her three kittens. "You see, children? The chickens have come home to roost. Crime never pays if you're dumb enough to get caught. Let this be a lesson to you."

On a better day I might have given them cats a few more lessons, but with the Department of Defense closing in on me, I just didn't have time.

I looked for a place to run but they had me cornered. One of the policemen had his shotgun pointed in my direction and one of the things you learn in security work is that arguing with a shotgun will mess up your coat and produce lead poisoning.

Instead of making a run for it, I sat down. The dogcatcher came creeping up with his net in the air, and if I'd made the slightest growl, I bet he would have jumped back into last week. But I didn't. He dropped the net around me and I was caught.

"Easy now, stand back, boys, I'm telling you this dog is out of his mind, he tried to tear my leg off back yonder and when I ran for the pickup he attacked one of my tires!"

Just then the guy in the T-shirt, the one who belonged to that sorry collection of cats, came out the gate and talked to the police. "Yeah, he's the one that tried to kill my cats. I thought there was something peculiar about that dog. And he's got rabies, huh? I suspected it all along, sure did."

They carried me to the dogcatcher's wagon and throwed me into the wire cage and locked the door. Then two or three of them stood around, staring at me and talking. The dogcatcher got a long stick and started poking at me with it. What was I supposed to do? I let him poke me a couple of times and then I bit the stick in half.

"Look at that! Did you see that? We got us a sick dog, boys, and did I tell you about how he tried to attack a child before y'all got here?"

"The heck he did!"

"Yes sir, and I'll tell you this, boys, and it comes from the bottom of my heart: if this town hadn't had a dogcatcher, half the little children on this end of town would be running around with hydrophobia right this minute!"

"Kids these days are bad enough without hydrophobia."

"That's right, Burt, and the next time that city council takes up the business of salaries, they better remember who goes out and saves the little children of this town from mad dogs."

One of the policemen bent down and looked at me. He made an ugly face, and I made one right back at him. "What do you do with a mad dog, Jimmy Joe?"

"Oh, we'll call the vet out to the pound tomorrow and he'll run a test."

"What's the test?"

"Cut off his head and send it to the state lab."

HUH? Cut . . . say, that didn't sound good at all. As a matter of fact, it sounded real bad. What the heck did they do if the test came out negative? I had a couple more questions I wanted answers to, but about that time Jimmy Joe Dogcatcher got into the pickup and hauled me off to the city dog pound.

It was on the south edge of town, on a lonely windblown hill. As we approached the place, I could hear the wind moaning through the chain link fences. Jimmy Joe backed up to a pen with a high fence around it and opened the gates so I could go into the pen.

He started poking me again with a stick. "Go on, you crazy devil, get out of there! This is the end of the road. No more biting innocent children for you, pal."

I don't know where he came up with that business about biting innocent children. I never bit an innocent child in my life, never even bit one who wasn't innocent. When you're Head of Ranch Security, you don't go around biting kids. Monsters, yes. Coyotes and coons and criminal dogs, yes. But kids, no.

Seemed to me the dogcatcher needed to have *his* head sent to the state lab, but nobody was interested in my opinion.

I went into the cell and laid down in a back corner. The dogcatcher slammed the door and stood there for a minute. "No collar, no dog tags, no name, no identification. We won't have to feed you long, old pup. You better have a good time tonight because tomorrow . . ."

He drew a finger across his throat and made a wicked sound. He flashed a big grin, got into his pickup, and drove away.

There was something about that dogcatcher I

didn't like.

Well, I lay there for a long time, listening to the wind and thinking about my situation. All at once I got the feeling that I was being watched. I raised my head, cut my eyes to both sides, perked my ears, and tested the wind.

Then I saw him: a basset hound in the cell next to mine. He had a long body, short, stubby legs, long drooping ears, and the saddest, most mournful face you could imagine.

"Howdy," he said in a slow-talking voice. "My name's Ralph."

"I'm Hank the Cowdog, Head of Ranch Security."

"Welcome to Death Row."

"Thanks. It's a real pleasure to be here."

"You really mean that?"

"What do you think?"

He sniffed his nose. "I 'spect not. You scared?"

"Maybe."

"I'd be scared if I was you. You really got hydrophobia like they said?"

"I don't know. Everybody thinks I do. Maybe I do." I told him the whole story, starting with the Ivory Dog Bar I ate at Maggie's place. Ralph didn't strike me as being real bright but I didn't have anything better to do than make conversation with him. It took my mind off my troubles.

It took me a while to tell the story. Ralph's eyelids were drooping when I started—I mean, I think that was just his normal condition. His whole face drooped: eyes, ears, jowls, everything. He was just a droopy kind of dog. Well, by the time I finished the story, he was asleep.

Kind of hacked me off, him falling asleep. I got up and sneaked over to the fence, put my mouth right down by his ear and yelled, "HEY!"

His whole body rose off the ground an inch or two and he opened his eyes. "Soap," he said.

"Well soap to you too! You shouldn't go around asking questions if you can't stay awake for the answers. Even a dog on Death Row deserves a little courtesy."

He blinked his eyes. "Soap's the answer."

"Yeah, but what's the question? It doesn't help to know the answer if you don't . . . what are you talking about?"

He pushed himself up and walked over to a water pan near the front of his cell. It was dark by this time and I could hear his claws clicking on the cement floor. He lapped up some water and came clicking back and sat down.

"Mouth gets dry when I talk too much." He ran his tongue over his chops and wiped off some excess water. "Seems to me you were the victim of a hoax."

"Not likely, friend. I've been in security work for a long time. I can smell a hoax half a mile away."

"Uh-huh, but it was soap."

"You said that before. It didn't make sense then and it don't make sense now."

"Well, if you'll shut up a minute, maybe I can explain."

I glared at him. "You're telling me to shut up, is that it?"

"Uh-huh, that's what I was driving at."

I sat down. "I can handle that. Tell me about soap."

"One time they was washing out the dog pens. They don't do it very often but this time they did. They had some little white bars that had 'Ivory' written on 'em."

"Okay, them was Ivory Dog Bars," I said. "The question here is, why would they use Ivory Dog Bars for cleaning the pen?"

Ralph stuck his nose against the chain link fence. "Because it was soap, ya dope."

"HUH?"

"You ain't got hydrophobia. You ate a bar of soap, is why you was foamin' at the mouth."

"Wait a minute, hold everything!" I sprang to my feet and began pacing. "It's coming clear now, all the clues are pointing in the same direction. At last the pieces of this puzzle are falling into place. I was duped into eating *a bar of soap,* which explains why it tasted so awful. I knew something wasn't right. Ivory Dog Bar indeed!

"It was soap, Ralph, don't you understand? They gave me soap, knowing it would produce the symptoms of hydrophobia. So all at once this case is leading in a new and startling direction, for you see, Ralph, they not only duped me, but also my sister, Maggie! Which brings us to the crux of the

matter, the throbbing heart of the mystery."

I whirled around and faced him. "The question now is, who are THEY and why did they want . . ."

Ralph was asleep again.

CHAPTER ELEVEN

Another
Case Is Solved

"**H**ey, wake up!"

Ralph's eyes fluttered open. "It was soap."

I paced back and forth in front of him. My mind was racing. "Of course it was soap, but that's only the tip of the ice cube. What we have here is a by-George conspiracy that could very well lead all the way to city hall! Do you understand what this means, Ralph?"

"Uh-huh."

"This could . . ." I stopped pacing and stared at him. "What do you mean 'uh-huh'?"

"I mean uh-huh, is what I mean."

I walked over to him. "Uh-huh meaning yes? You understand what this means? You're trying to tell me that you've figgered it out?"

107

"Uh-huh."

"Who's Head of Ranch Security?"

"You."

"And who's just a sad sack, jailbird hound?"

"Me."

"And you expect me to believe that you know who poisoned me?"

"Yup."

"All right, smart guy, I'll listen, and it better be good."

"Well," said Ralph, "sounds to me like your sister gave you some soap to eat."

"We've already established that, Ralph."

"Because you gave her daughter fleas."

"Huh?"

"And because she wanted you to go home."

"Go home? Me?" I studied on that for a while. "There's only one thing wrong with your theory, Ralph. It's a house of cards built on the idea that I'm not welcome at my sister's place. Remove that one card and the entire structure comes crashing down. No, Ralph, your theory is not only wrong, it's incorrect."

He shrugged. "Okay, whatever you think."

"It wasn't a stupid idea, Ralph, and it shows that you're trying."

"Well . . ."

"I'm sorry."

"Yeah, I'm sorry too, 'cause tomorrow morning they're gonna cut your head off and send it to Austin, all because you ate a bar of soap. That's sure too bad."

I cut my eyes from side to side. "You've got a point there. It doesn't do much good to solve a case if you lose your head in the process. Which brings us to another matter."

"What's that?"

I ran my eyes over the steel and cement. "I'm going to bust out of here tonight."

"It's made perty stout."

"Pretty stout but not ralph enough, Tout . . . uh Rout . . . uh Ralph. When you get to know me better, you'll learn that I have my ways of escaping."

"Well, okay. Reckon I ought to move out of the way?"

"That might be a good idea. Move to the back of your cell, just in case. There's no sense in taking chances."

He pushed himself up and yawned. "It sure was nice meetin' you, Hank, and best of luck."

"And the same goes for you, my friend. We'll see you down the road."

We waved good-bye. I watched him amble off to the back of his cell and I felt a lump in my throat.

I mean, there's something special about friendships made in prison. You just don't forget the guys you've met on Death Row.

I gave Ralph time to take cover and made a few warm-up runs around my cell. Then I turned to the south and focused all my attention on the chain link fence.

Destroying a chain link fence with steel posts set in concrete wasn't going to be easy, but then life itself wasn't easy and being Head of Ranch Security wasn't easy and getting my head cut off and sent to the state lab wasn't easy, so there you are. What's easy in this life isn't necessarily . . . I've lost my train of thought.

I jogged in place for a moment, took three deep breaths, and glanced up at the stars. The time was approximately 1:34 a.m. With any luck at all, this nightmare would be over in fifteen minutes and I would be on my way back to the ranch.

All at once my highly conditioned body stiffened from nose to tail, as I concentrated on being an arrow, a battering ram, an artillery shell, a guided missile. And then I sprang forward, gathering speed with every step, and by the time I reached the fence I had attained maximum velocity.

I crashed into the fence and suddenly the night silence was filled with the sounds of destruction—

the snap and groan of steel under stress and also the snap and groan of various parts of my body.

When I regained consciousness I was lying on the floor of my cell. A new day was dawning in the east and Ralph was in the cell beside me, looking down with drooping eyes, drooping jowls, and drooping ears.

I sat up and shook the vapors out of my head. "Where am I?"

"You're still on Death Row."

"What happened?"

"Oh, you hit the fence and it didn't tear down."

"And I've been unconscious all this time?"

"Yup."

I looked closer at Ralph. "How did you get into my cell?"

"Oh, just opened a couple of gates and came on in. I didn't figger you'd mind."

"No, I don't mind at all. In fact," I tried to roll the stiffness out of my neck, "I appreciate it. Thanks."

"You're welcome. It wasn't much. I figgered you might want some company, this being your last day and everything."

I pushed myself up and walked around. "Yes, this is the last day, isn't it? I tried to escape and failed, and now I must pay the price of failure."

"Perty expensive, ain't it?"

"Yes, very expensive. Well, it's all come down to this one day, hasn't it, Ralph?"

"Yup."

"My entire life, my career as Head of Ranch Security, my adventures, my friendships, the many women I've shared my heart with. And all the crazy little incidents along the way, Ralph, they come rushing back to me now. Do you have any idea how I must feel at this moment?"

"Nope."

"Well, thanks for trying. And thanks for being a true friend. And thanks for sharing these moments with me. And thanks," I choked up a little bit, "and thanks for being a dog."

"You're welcome."

I had to turn away from him. I didn't want him to see me . . . well, you understand. I looked off to the east. "Just look at it, Ralph. Have you ever seen a bigger, redder sun or a more beautiful sunset?"

"I think it's a sun *rise*."

"That's what I meant. Did I say sunset?"

"Yup."

"Well, whatever. The point is that it's beautiful, but an even deeper point, and the one I want to emphasize . . ." I stared at Ralph. "You walked into my cell, through that door?"

"Yup."

"How did you do that?"

"Just pushed the latch up with my nose. It was perty easy."

I had to sit down. "Wait a minute. You opened your cell door and . . . why didn't you escape?"

He scratched at a flea on his ear. "Oh, I got no place special to go. I been stayin' out here for two years. It's kind of like home now."

"You're not condemned? You're not on Death Row?"

"Well, sorta, but me and Jimmy Joe get along all right, and I never had hydrophobia."

"Well, I never did either but . . . what time does Jimmy Joe come out here in the mornings?"

"Oh about ten minutes from now, maybe less."

"All right, Ralph. I have one last question, and I want you to think about it very carefully before you give me an answer."

"Okay."

"Is there some reason why I can't walk out my cell door and escape?"

"Let me think about that." He closed his eyes and went into deep concentration.

I waited for five minutes. In the distance I heard a pickup motor, and suddenly I realized that Ralph was asleep.

"Ralph, wake up!" His eyes floated open.

"Hurry, give me your answer before it's too late!"

"What was the question?"

"Is there any reason why I can't walk out that door and escape?"

He rubbed his chin with a paw. "No, by gollies, it ought to work."

"That's all I wanted to know." I sprinted to the door, gave it a push with my nose, and it swung open. The pickup was coming closer. I looked back at Ralph. "Just one more last question."

"Okay."

"Why didn't you tell me you knew how to open this door?"

He frowned and squinted one eye. "Well, you didn't ask. And I guess it just slipped my mind. Don't that beat it all?"

"Yes, Ralph, that beats it all and it almost got my head cut off. Well, this is good-bye, and thanks for nuthin'."

"You're sure welcome, Hank. So long."

Just as the dogcatcher's pickup pulled up, I shot out of my cell and headed for freedom. This would have been a natural place to bring the story to a close with a happy ending, only Jimmy Joe Dogcatcher saw what had happened and took off after me.

You see, no happy ending is real until the end has ended happily.

CHAPTER TWELVE

The End Ends Happily After All

The dogcatcher must have been pretty unhappy when he pulled up to the dog pens and found his old pal Ralph sitting in Death Row. As I dashed off across the pasture, I heard him squall and beller.

Then he jumped into his pickup, spun the tires, and came after me.

I had supposed he would follow the road, see, and that would give me a little advantage and a head start. Nope. He came right behind me, and off we went across the pasture.

I ducked under a barbed wire fence and thought that would slow him down, since he would have to hunt for a gate. Nope. He built a new gate, just by George rammed it and drove right through it.

115

Then I came to a draw that ran through the pasture. It was kind of steep on the sides and bumpy in the middle, and I figgered that would slow him down. Nope. He derned near tore the axles off the pickup, but he made it through and kept coming.

And then he started shooting! That's right, had a pistol out the left window, drove with one hand and fired with the other. That seems a little radical, him shooting at me right on the outskirts of town, until you stop and remember that he still thought I had hydrophobia, and then it still seems a little radical.

It appeared to me my best lick was to get over to the highway. Surely if I got around cars and people, that nutty dogcatcher would hold his fire. Then all I would have to worry about would be him running over me with his pickup.

So I changed course and headed west and struck the highway right in front of Waterhole 83, the place where Loper and Slim bought their soda pop and chewing tobacco. I'd been there a time or two.

Sure nuff, once I got around the highway Jimmy Joe had to put away his artillery. I dashed across, a step or two ahead of a semi-truck, and made a run for the Waterhole. I went around the

116

back side just as Jimmy Joe roared into the parking lot. He screeched his tires and followed.

My plan at this point was to run around the Waterhole until Jimmy Joe ran out of gas, but when I came around the south side I saw a familiar faded red pickup sitting out front. Just as Slim opened his door and touched the ground with a booted spur, or a spurred boot I guess I should say, I dived in and hit the floorboard.

"What . . . where . . . good grief, it's you again!"

There wasn't a great deal of warmth in Slim's

statement. "Good grief, it's you again" sort of recognized the basic facts of the situation but was a long distance, emotionally speaking, from "By golly, Hank, it's great to see you again!"

But of course you have to remember that I had left the ranch under the shadow of controversy, so to speak.

Well, I whapped my tail on the floorboard and gave him one of my most pitiful looks. I couldn't tell if it was working or not, and just then the dogcatcher came roaring through the parking lot and screeched to a halt.

I made my best attempt to melt into the floormat. I mean, I was by George hugging the floor.

"Say," Jimmy Joe yelled, "you see a sorry looking dog go running through here?"

Slim shot me a glance, slammed the door, and walked over to the other pickup. "Yalp."

"Where'd he go?"

Slim leaned his elbow on the pickup and pointed off to the north. "See that milk truck there, says Nowlin's Dairy?"

"Right, yeah, okay, thanks, I'll run him down." And he roared off after the milk truck.

Slim went into the Waterhole and came out with a sack of sunflower seeds. He got in and looked down at me. "I didn't lie to him. He asked if I'd seen a sorry looking dog and I said yes. I didn't say you were in that milk truck, didn't even mean to suggest it. He just jumped to conclusions."

He gave me a wink and we headed south toward the ranch. After we'd gone a few miles, I worked up the courage to sit in the seat and, you know, let the wind blow across my ears. Always did enjoy that.

When we crossed the cattleguard that put us

back on the ranch, Slim pushed his hat back on his head, looked at me and sighed.

"Hank, Sally May's gonna scalp me when she finds out I brought you back out here. In fact," he slammed on the brakes and opened the door, "why don't you walk in to headquarters alone. I've got enough trouble without being associated with your lousy record."

Lousy Record! I couldn't believe my ears. What about all those long nights on patrol, all the years . . . oh well.

I jumped out into the road. Slim didn't drive off right away but sat there looking at me. He even grinned. "Hank, I'm kind of glad you're back, and I'll be derned if I can find a reason for it. You're as dumb as any dog I ever met and you cause more trouble around here than you're worth."

All at once he started laughing. "Broke into the house and ate the T-bone steaks right off the table! You sorry devil, we should have shot you while we were mad." He shook his head. "See you to the house, old pup."

And he drove away. Well, what can you say about that kind of welcome-home? On the one hand, I think Slim meant every word he said. On the other hand, his words weren't entirely flattering, so there you are.

He'd let me out on the country road, just north and west of the house, right there by Spook Canyon where the road runs through the horse pasture. I started to the house and ran into the horses. Must have been twelve of them right there in a bunch.

I was feeling pretty good—I mean, who wouldn't? I had survived a case of Soap Hydrophobia, I had escaped from a cell on Death Row, and I had smuggled my bad self out of town just one step ahead of the posse. And I was home again!

Shucks, it was a great day. I was full of vinegar and oil and the other spices of life, I wanted to run and play and rejoice, and just by George tell everybody that it was great to be alive and home.

So I marched up to the horses. Thought it might be fun to put on a little demonstration of cowdog skills—you know, round 'em up into a bunch, head 'em down toward the corrals, stop 'em, loose-herd 'em, in other words a little practice run, just for the pure fun of it.

"All right, you crowbaits, the chief executive is back on the ranch! Form up into a group and move out to the corrals, and stand by for further orders."

They formed up into a group all right but they went in the wrong direction. Instead of heading down toward the corrals, the scoundrels came running toward ME. I retreated a couple of steps and they kept on coming. I broke into a run and they kept coming. I ran all the way to the corral with them horses right on my tail, kicking and bucking and snorting.

Which just goes to show that we cowdogs have many tricks in our bags. Oftentimes the best way to move horses into a corral is to make them think you want to *drive* them, see, then let them drive *you*.

We call this "Reverse Psychology" and we use it a lot, especially on horses because they're very ornery and stubborn and willful, also dangerous, and I never did get much pleasure out of messing with a bunch of stupid horses.

But it was still a great day, so good that even horses couldn't mess it up. I marched through the corrals, noticed there were a couple of steers in the sick pen so I made my rounds there, got 'em up on their feet, stirred 'em, checked their noses and eyes and other technical medical stuff that most ordinary readers wouldn't understand—well, just for an example, I had a steer once that had eardroopus, redeyestacosis, and drynoserosis.

Handling heavy technical terms is something a good cowdog does every day, but as I say we don't expect the ordinary reader . . . I think I've already covered this.

After I'd made my hospital rounds, I went padding through the corrals, feeling like a million, when all of a sudden I saw something up ahead that caught my eye.

There was a stock tank up ahead, see, right there in the fenceline between the alley and the side lot. Pete the Barncat was perched up on the edge of the tank, all bunched up in such a way that he had all four paws resting on a very small ledge. That's something a cat can do. It's a balancing trick that doesn't require any brains.

His tail was high in the air, flicking back and forth in a slow rhythm. He was looking into the water and—get this—talking to someone! That's right. Well, naturally I had to postpone his daily whipping so I could listen.

Oh, you're so handsome! My heavens! My stars!
My goodness, my gracious, my gravy, my gosh
You're the best looking cat,
I'm inclined to think that
I'm in love with you, dear,
Can you see, can you hear
My heart beating and pounding
And thumping and sounding

The incredible love that I feel for myself?

I can hardly explain it,
It hurts like a bayonet,
This incredible love that I feel for myself.

It's as gold as a carrot,
I'm not sure I can bear it,
This incredible love that I feel for myself.

I see in reflections,
In every direction,
The incredible love that I feel for myself.

Dear cat, you're so handsome,
You're worth a king's ransom!
Oh Pete, I'm in love with yourself!

If you recall, I had spent several hours on patrol in the alleys of Twitchell, Texas, but in all that time I hadn't encountered garbage to compare with *this*. But it confirmed what I had always said about cats: They may not be the smartest animals in the world, but they sure are the dumbest.

Well, Petie Pie was so busy saying love poems to himself that he didn't hear me sneaking up behind him. And moments later, I enjoyed one of the greatest honors of my career. While Pete was poised on the edge of the tank, looking at his reflection in the water, I slipped up behind him, slapped him across the backside with a paw, and sent him flying into the stock tank.

And as you know, Pete HATES water worse than sin. It was a DELICIOUS moment for me, watching him crawl out wet and mussed while at the same time remembering the trouble he had

caused me with that fraud about the End of the World.

"There you go, cat, just a little reminder that the Head of Ranch Security is back. Take note and beware."

I left the cat sputtering and spitting and went on through the corrals, through the front lot, past the saddle shed, and on toward the gas tanks. There, in the shade of the big Chinese elms, I saw Drover. He was crouched low to the ground, stalking a cricket. He heard me coming and looked up.

"Oh boy, Hank's back!" He started jumping up and down. "Gosh, I'm glad to see you. The nights were awful scary while you were gone."

"Pretty bad, huh?"

"Just awful! The first night you were gone, the coons broke into the feed barn, and the second night a coyote came right up to the house, and he howled, Hank, and called me nasty names."

"Did, huh. What did you do?"

"Oh," Drover looked up at the sky. "I barked at him . . . from the machine shed. I barked at him once or twice . . . I intended to bark at him once or twice . . . maybe I didn't bark at all, but my bad leg was giving me trouble, Hank and . . ."

"I've got the picture, son. In other words, while

I was gone things went to pot, rot, rack, and ruin."

"Well, they sure went to pot and rack . . . and maybe to rot and ruin too. I guess you're right, Hank."

"Just as I suspected. Well Drover, there's an important lesson about life to be learned from all this." His eyes widened and he waited for the lesson. "It was on the tip of my tongue just a second ago." I paced back and forth, probing my memory. "And it was very, very important." I probed deeper. "But at the moment I can't remember what it was."

"Gosh, that's too bad."

"But we can take comfort in knowing there are important lessons to be learned, and in the meantime let's get some sleep. Because, Drover . . ." I glanced over both shoulders and dropped my voice to a whisper. "Tonight will be another night. The evil forces will rise again from the ground. And WE will be there to oppose them!"

Have you read all of Hank's adventures?

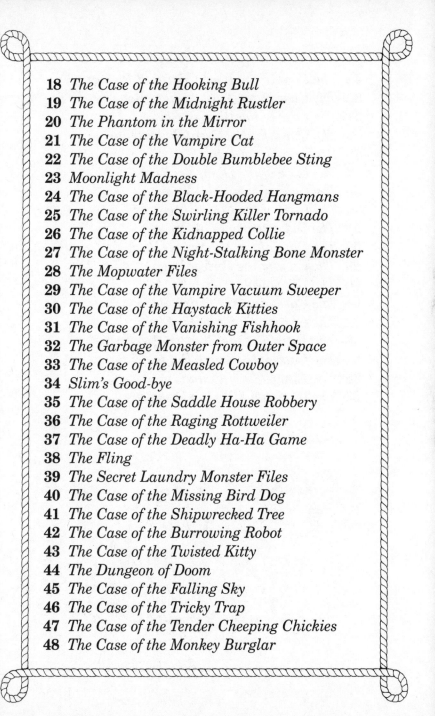

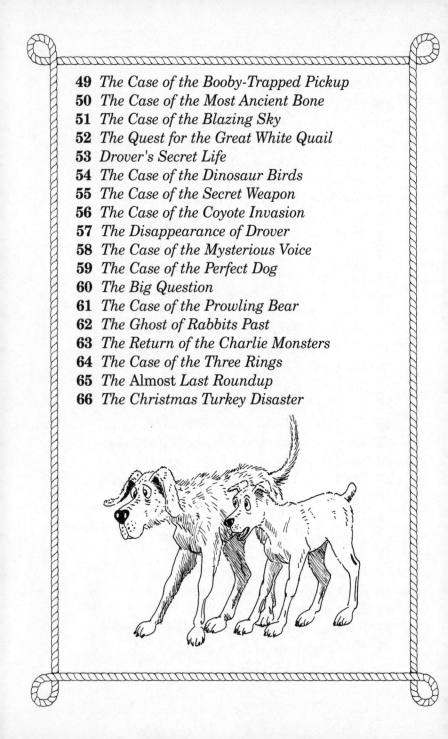

The following activities are samples from *The Hank Times*, the official newspaper of Hank's Security Force. Do not write on these pages unless this is your book. Even then, why not just find a scrap of paper?

For more games and activities like these, be sure to check out Hank's official website at **www.hankthecowdog.com**!

"Photogenic" Memory Quiz

We all know that Hank has a "photogenic" memory—being aware of your surroundings is an important quality for a Head of Ranch Security. Now you can test your powers of observation.

How good is your memory? Look at the illustration on page 32 and try to remember as many things about it as possible. Then turn back to this page and see how many questions you can answer.

1. Was Sally May holding a Mop, a Broom, or a Rake?

2. What was in the window: a Plant, Cactus, or Flowers?

3. What month was it on the calendar: May, June, July, or Wednesday?

4. Was Hank retreating under: a Table, a Chair or a Couch?

5. What was in the jar: Honey, Jelly, or Jam?

6. How many of Hank's eyes could you see: 1, 2, or all 3?

"Rhyme Time"

W hat if Hank's sister, Maggie, tired of Hank's visit and decided to go look for a job? What kind of jobs could she do?

Make a rhyme using the name MAG that would relate to her new job possibilities below.

1. Mag makes a sack for people to carry groceries home in.

2. Mag teaches a class teaching puppies how to act happy.

3. Mag gripes, complains and pesters someone all day.

4. Mag sells old cloth pieces used to clean up messes.

5. Mag teaches people how to tell if a person is choking.

6. Mag talks all the time about how super and great Hank is.

7. Mag teaches you what to do after you've zigged.

8. Mag creates a new kind of jigsaw type puzzle.

9. Mag invents a game where someone is IT, and everyone runs around trying not to get touched by that person.

Answers:

1. Mag BAG   4. Mag RAG   7. Mag ZAG
2. Mag WAG   5. Mag GAG   8. Mag JAG
3. Mag NAG   6. Mag BRAG   9. Mag TAG

"Word Maker"

Try making words from the names below. Make up to twenty words with as many letters as possible.

Then count the total number of letters used in all of the words you made. See how well you did using the security rankings below.

MAGGIE AND RALPH

55-61   You spend too much time with J.T. Cluck and the chickens.

62-67   You are showing some real Security Force potential.

68-72   You have earned a spot on our ranch security team.

73+   Wow! You rank up there as a top-of-the-line cowdog.

John R. Erickson, a former cowboy, has written numerous books for both children and adults and is best known for his acclaimed *Hank the Cowdog* series. He lives and works on his ranch in Perryton, Texas, with his family.

Gerald L. Holmes has illustrated numerous cartoons and textbooks in addition to the *Hank the Cowdog* series. He lives in Perryton, Texas.